CAN'T HURRY LOVE

LIBBY WATERFORD

This is a work of fiction. Names, places, organizations, and events are either products of the author's imagination or are used entirely fictitiously.

Copyright © 2021 by Libby Waterford
All rights reserved.

No part of this book may be reproduced in any form or by any electronic or mechanical means, including information storage and retrieval systems, without written permission from the author, except for the use of brief quotations in a book review.

ALSO BY LIBBY WATERFORD

Sawyer's Cove: The Reboot

Take Two

Take a Bow

Take it All

Take a Chance

Hot Take in Steamy Shorts: A Kissed by Romance Anthology

Take Another Look in A Kiss at Midnight: A Kissed by Romance Collaboration

Never a Bride

Can't Help Falling in Love

Can't Make You Love Me

Can't Fight This Feeling

Can't Hurry Love

Weston Reunion

Flirting with Her Professor

Her Reunion Fling

Falling for Her Ex

For Julie

CHAPTER 1

KATE

What's the name of that place with the thing that you said I had to visit, Nicole?

NICOLE

The Cloisters?

KATE

That's it. Oliver's taking me there tomorrow.

NICOLE

Jelly! I miss New York so much sometimes.

KATE

I'm beginning to see why. I thought it could never live up to my expectations, but it's even better.

ROSIE

That's because you are there with someone you love. 🤍

KATE

That might have something to do with it. 😊

OPHELIA

Who's up for the farmers market tomorrow?

LANI

I can probably meet you there.

ROSIE

Working, sorry

NICOLE

Ricky & I will be in the mountains.

OPHELIA

Oh I forgot about your camping trip.

ROSIE

You & Ricky are going camping?? Who are you & what have you done with Nicole?

LANI

Don't freak, Rosie. If it involves a cabin & electricity, it's not camping.

NICOLE

But we'll be unplugged, I swear. We're doing one of those digital detox weekends.

KATE

Whose idea was that?

OPHELIA

That doesn't exactly sound like either your or Ricky's idea of a good time.

NICOLE

Technically it was a wedding present from Ricky's aunt. But it will be good for us. No texting, podcasts, social media or news for 48 hours.

ROSIE

That actually sounds pretty nice

LANI

What will you do to fill the time? 

NICOLE

I'm sure we'll think of something.

ROSIE

Maybe I'll look into that for Gus's birthday.

OPHELIA

Lani, is it OK if Jamie comes with tomorrow?

LANI

Sure

Why wouldn't it?

OPHELIA

IDK I feel bad that we're a package deal these days.

NICOLE

Honey, you were a package deal before you figured out you were in love with each other.

OPHELIA

Fair point

LANI

You know you all don't have to tiptoe around me. Just because you've all coupled up doesn't mean I'm not happy doing my sexy single gal thing.

Besides, someone has to carry on the single lady flag. And make fun of you all, too.

NICOLE

…

LANI

Don't say it, Nicole

NICOLE

Say what?

LANI

You were going to say something about how I shouldn't talk because I could be next. Sorry to disappoint but there's no way I'm going to be felled by cupid's arrow like the rest of you.

Gotta go, I'm heading to Wild Child for a caffeine infusion.

ROSIE

Careful, you could end up with that cute barista. I love a good coffee shop romance.

KATE

Imagine, free coffee for life!

OPHELIA

I thought you were seeing the guy with the dog from the farmers market.

LANI

The guy with the dog was weeks ago & while I might flirt I like the coffee at Wild Child too much to actually get involved with an employee.

NICOLE

You really are the smartest one of all of us, Lani

LANI

Now you're catching on 

* * *

BEVERLY THE REALTOR

Your offer on the house has been officially submitted. Now you can relax until we hear from the sellers.

LANI

Relax? Don't you mean bite my nails until we hear from them? 

It's out of your hands. We put together a respectable offer. It's Friday. Have fun this weekend. Take your mind off it. We won't hear anything until Monday, probably.

I want to know the second you hear.

Of course!

And thnx for everything

I have a good feeling about this. This is your house.

Pretty sure you're only saying that because you're sick of showing me places.

Never! This is it, darling.

I hope the sellers agree.

CHAPTER 2
LANI

Fridays at Winesap Design tend to be light—except when they're not. Today my schedule isn't too crazy-packed. I have a marketing meeting later, but Nicole's finally out of the office, having headed off to her dreaded digital detox weekend after a flurry of last-minute emails and texts. I'm looking forward to a weekend of radio silence even if she isn't.

Waiting for Beverly to let me know if the sellers accepted my offer on my dream house has me jumping at every notification. She wants me to relax and try to put it out of my mind, so I grab my sketchbook. Drawing is one of the only things that helps me turn off my brain for a while.

I rinse out my travel mug and walk the half block from the office to Wild Child Café. I'll get some drawing time in while I recharge with a midday latte and pointedly not think about the possibility of soon becoming a bona fide homeowner.

It's one of those perfect mid-September afternoons that proves I live in the best place on Earth. Santa Barbara is rarely too hot or too cold. The foggy days are pleasantly fresh while the hot summer days are dry, not muggy. There's always something blooming, from roses to jacaranda trees. It's similar in that way to where I grew up on Kauai. I'm grateful for the umpteenth time that Nicole's trust fund allowed us to set up shop in a walkable part of town close to every amenity, including Wild Child.

I burst through the doors and Jayson greets me with a chin lift. "The usual?"

"Yes, please."

I hand him the travel mug and he starts my latte. The pastry case is conspicuously bare and I groan in disappointment. "Don't tell me you're out of the macadamia nut cookies."

"Sorry, Lani, someone just bought the last one." Jayson nods toward the person behind me.

I whirl around to cast a stink eye at the cookie usurper. There's only one other person in the shop and he's sitting in my favorite window seat, the one closest to an outlet for charging. It's a twentysomething white guy, sitting in front of an open laptop. Half a macadamia nut cookie sits on a napkin next to it. I'm about to go to my second-favorite menu item when the sticker on the back of his computer catches my eye. It's a black and white decal of two familiar characters, a little boy and a little girl. I recognize them from the children's books I have relegated to a hard-to-reach corner bookshelf in my apartment. Reed and Lucy are not especially well-known characters outside of readers with ages in the single digits, though there are five books, and counting, in the series. Why would a grown man have that particular sticker displayed on the back of his silver laptop?

I look at him more closely. He's got sandy-brown hair and a hint of a baby face, open and unlined. He's wearing jeans and a T-shirt screen-printed with the *Dark Side of the Moon* cover art. There's a leather strap tied around his right wrist. His black leather boots are well-worn, and the backpack that hangs over the back of his chair looks like it has just as many miles on it. He's got his eyes on the laptop, but he's not typing. I wonder if he's one of those people who go to a café to pretend to work but watch trending videos on the free Wi-Fi instead.

You would think I'd already know if he's that type of person, considering I know that his eyes, if they looked at me instead of at the computer screen, would be platinum gray, and his voice, if he spoke to me, would be deeper than his baby face would indicate.

Now I know why he's got those characters on his computer. He's Reed Bennet, the author of the Reed and Lucy children's book series.

He's also my husband.

And now he's looking right at me.

"Lani?"

I might have wondered if he'd engineered this meeting except for the clear astonishment on his face.

"What are you doing here, Reed?" It's not original, but it captures the spirit of the million questions zinging around my brain.

"I'm working."

"Okay." That doesn't explain his presence here, in Wild Child. Or Santa Barbara, for that matter.

"Wow, I had no idea—I mean, I knew you—yeah, I didn't think—" He blows out a harsh breath and laughs dryly. "I imagined I might see you, but I didn't know it would be this hard to—"

"Say words?"

"Yeah, that."

"What are you doing here in Santa Barbara?"

"Book tour. I write children's books."

I make a noncommittal noise.

"Also, my agent—well, he's my friend, too—Kingston— you'd like him—he thought it would be good for me to have a change of scene. I'm working on a book and it's not going very well. So I thought I'd spend a few days here. Why not?"

I can think of about a billion reasons but can't seem to find the words to communicate any of them right now. Besides my shock at seeing Reed, I'm most shaken by the fact that he doesn't resemble The Boy much at all.

The Boy was what I called Reed Bennet before I knew his name, when he was just an eighteen-year-old kid in my psych class at UCSB. I was two years older, fancied myself a world more sophisticated. The last time I saw him he was twenty-two and looked it. He seems to have grown since then, his thick upper arms straining the sleeves of his T-shirt. The leather strap around his wrist used to fit more loosely. Now it's taut around his corded muscular forearm. His hair's a little shorter, a little darker, a little spikier. His nose is still a bit round, as are his cheeks, a trace of The Boy I used to know. But everything else seems to be all man.

Dammit.

Suddenly I'm glad I wore my new saffron-yellow high-waisted linen trousers and a cream-colored blouse instead of dressing down for casual Friday. I'm put together to my usual high standards, but I can't help but be slightly self-conscious about the fine lines etched into the creases next to my eyes, even though he probably can't see them from halfway across the room. I've been blessed with my Hawaiian mother's clear dark olive skin and her thick black hair, but since I turned thirty, nothing about me is quite as elastic as it once was.

But Reed looks indisputably good. Scruffy, but good.

Despite surprising the shit out of each other, he now seems to be acting as if we run into each other all the time, all calm and matter-of-fact while I feel like I might need to breathe into a paper bag or eat about a dozen of those macadamia nut cookies. If he hadn't eaten the last one.

"Here's your latte."

I turn around to find Jayson holding out my mug.

"Oh thanks. Yeah." I put down my sketchbook to grab it, flustered.

Jayson frowns. "Everything okay?" His gaze flits over my shoulder to Reed. "He bothering you?" he asks in a low voice.

Yes.

"No, it's fine. Despite taking my cookie, he's a...friend."

Jayson shrugs and retreats behind the counter. I take a shaky sip of my coffee. The familiar flavor anchors me and reminds me I'm on my own turf. I have people at my back. Reed is the interloper. I straighten my shoulders.

"Okay, so you're here. Great. Well, have a good stay."

"Wait. Can you join me?" Reed looks at the empty chair across from him.

"I've got a meeting." Not for two more hours.

"Do you have dinner plans?"

"Dinner plans?" I wrack my brain. I don't have plans, unless making myself a salad and finishing my mystery novel count.

"Is the Italian place with the outrageous garlic bread still there?"

"Yes." I feel the urge to start asserting myself instead of just reacting to him. "But there's a place a block over that's much better. Olio e Limone. I'll meet you there at seven."

"Do we need a reservation?"

"I'll make one."

"Okay, thanks."

I manage to pay Jayson without looking over my shoulder to see if Reed's disappeared. Maybe he was a figment of my imagination. But when I do turn around, no such luck. I have to walk past his table to get outside. It feels like a trap, like Reed is lying in wait for me to come near enough for him to grab me. But that's silly. I'm not afraid of him. I'm...unsettled.

Seeing the person you happen to be married to for the first time in six years can do that to you.

I clutch my mug in both hands and march out of the shop.

A couple comes in as I'm leaving, and they hold the door for me so I don't have to let go of my coffee, my lifeline, my defense against unwanted complications. Reed Bennet has been one unwanted complication after another from the moment I met him.

"See you tonight, Lani."

I don't answer as I scoot out the door as fast as I can without it seeming as if I'm running away.

CHAPTER 3

REED

I didn't plan running into Lani, but I would be lying if I said I hadn't mapped out where she works and chosen a rental apartment a few blocks away. I don't know where she lives, so it was the closest I could come to putting myself in her path and hoping the universe would take care of the rest.

Score one for the universe, because I've been in California for less than twenty-four hours and I already have a date with my wife.

It's not as if I don't have her phone number. I mean, I think I do, if it's the same one she had when we were together, two dumb college kids who thought we had our whole lives figured out. My number's different, though. When I got to New York I couldn't afford my plan. After I switched to a cheap phone, I was careful to save Lani's information, entering it in diligently, careful not to transpose any digits.

I haven't called her once in the four years since I did that. But I held onto her number anyway.

When it comes to Lani, I have a hard time letting go.

Seeing her in the flesh was wild. I could have taken a bit more care with myself before heading out for a caffeine fix and an unproductive work session. I was wearing my shabbiest clothes. Bedhead and stubble don't do me any favors.

I stare at the door for way too long after Lani leaves the café, then pack it in. It's not like I was getting any work done. All I've successfully managed to accomplish today is eat a surprisingly good cookie.

On my way out, the guy who'd waited on both me and Lani earlier waves me over.

"Hey, man, you're a friend of Lani's, right?"

It's a spectacular understatement as well as more than I would have claimed to be yesterday, so I nod.

"She left this here. I can give it to her when she comes in, but that probably won't be until next week, so I thought if you were going to see her?" He holds up a black notebook—no, a sketchbook.

I take it without hesitation. "No problem, I'll give it to her."

"Thanks, dude."

I take the long way back to my rental, Lani's sketchbook secured in my backpack with my laptop, my face turned toward the late afternoon sun as it edges its way to the horizon, the tang of the ocean fresh and clean in my lungs.

Santa Barbara hasn't changed much since I was last here, still tidily beautiful, with its appealing mix of Spanish colonial and modern architecture. I especially appreciate the wide sidewalks and the green trees and the way the sun reaches all the way to the sidewalk after four years of living in a third-floor walk-up in Queens with a revolving door of harmless if antisocial roommates, three guys to a single bathroom.

My ground-floor studio rental here feels palatial by comparison. I tap the code into the keypad that grants me access to my temporary home. Even though I've been here for a single night and I'm leaving in a few days, this space already feels more like home than I ever felt in New York. I'm more certain than ever I'm making the right choice by moving back here. I still have to work out some of the details—okay, all of the details—but when Kingston talked my publisher into arranging this California book tour, I knew it was partly because he was sick of my talking about going back to California and wanted to nudge me into actually doing something about it. Kingston's excellent at nudging.

Now that I'm here, I know this is what I want: palm trees and the beach, sunny sidewalks, and traffic and wildfire danger and overpriced real estate. Lani being here has nothing to do with it, I swear.

I set Lani's sketchbook down on the bed so I won't forget it, plug my computer in to charge, then grab a quick shower. I take the time to shave. I have to stoop to see my face in the tiny mirror over the sink, but it's worth it. Lani looked like a model today—I've definitely got to up my game. She was always out of my league, and while that is undoubtedly still true, I'm capable of cleaning up enough that she won't regret being seen with me in public.

My phone rings as I'm combing through my suitcase for something to wear. I packed for a week on the road and informal bookstore events—jeans, T-shirts, a few flannel button-downs. My uniform, in other words.

"Kingston, hang on." I switch the phone to speaker mode.

Kingston's voice booms, bold and brash from a continent away. "How's sunny Cali treating you?"

"No one here calls it Cali," I say. "And so far, so weird. I ran into Lani. We're getting dinner."

"Tell me everything."

Kingston is one of the only people in my life who knows the truth: that Lani and I eloped right before I got a space off the waitlist at the creative writing MFA program of my dreams. I left California for Iowa and to write the Great American Novel. Lani didn't come with me.

"It wasn't a complete train wreck." I deem my dark blue flannel shirt the dressiest. I speak in the general direction of my phone while I button up my button-down. Language is so weird. I love it. "I could have spilled coffee all over myself. Or her. But it was still awkward as fuck."

"Did you know she was going to be there?"

"No. I searched for 'coffee shop Wi-Fi' and that was the nearest place. I was working."

"You were working?" Kingston's tone is insultingly skeptical. Problem is, he's not wrong. "On the book?"

"Well, I was on my computer, anyway." After nearly four years as my agent, he knows me too well.

"But she agreed to go to dinner with you, so it couldn't have gone too badly."

"I guess." I hadn't exactly expected her to agree, but then she'd set the location, the time. She didn't give me an extra spare second, just barked out orders and expected me to follow them. Kind of hot, to be honest.

"How did she look?" Kingston asks, as if he can tell where my mind is going.

"She looked...put together." She'd been glossy as a silk flower in a yellow and white ensemble complete with shit-kicking white suede heels. She looked like a cheerful domina-trix with her unsmiling, brightly painted mouth, iron-straight hair, and shellacked red fingernails. The Lani I remember always dressed with care, but she was softer, less lacquered. Her nails were always painted a different color, loud teal or hot pink. Today they were crimson, to match her lips.

"What does that mean? I can't believe you've never even shown me her picture. I could find one online, probably."

"She doesn't do social media." Should I throw some gel on my hair or will it look like I'm trying too hard? She saw me at my most casual this afternoon, so a little gel should be okay.

"Seriously? I thought she was a businesswoman."

"The design company she works for has all that stuff, but she doesn't have personal accounts."

"And you know this how?"

"Never mind." It's not like I actively cyber stalk my estranged wife or anything. But since I have to be on all those platforms to promote my books, I noticed when one of our old college friends posted about a new venture called Winesap Design, with a picture of a beaming Lani and a perky blonde in front of a warehouse-type building with the company's name emblazoned on the side. I read the press release, so proud of Lani for using her hard-won MBA to launch a brand-new business in typical badass fashion.

"So, what does she look like?"

"She's beautiful."

"You're a writer," Kingston says with a smile in his voice. "You can do a shade better than beautiful."

"She's skinny, but strong. Average height. Her nose is wide and her lips are generous and her eyes are dark and she has a mole on her left cheek under her eye. She used to pretend to get annoyed when I'd call it her beauty mark. I think she's always kind of hated it, but I think it's sexy."

"There you go. Way to dig deep, Reed. I hope dinner goes well. For your sake."

"Why shouldn't it?" I can't forget the way she'd been entirely nonplussed at my appearance. I'd envisioned our reunion dozens of times. Sometimes in my imagination she's angry, cries maybe, takes out six years of anger on me in one passionate moment. Other times I imagine she's pleased to see me, shy but smiling, perhaps offering me a hug. Then I remember she was never much into public displays of affection.

"You've got a deadline," he reminds me, unnecessarily. "Isn't this trip about freeing some of your creative juices? So go on, get juiced."

"Why does everything you say sound vaguely dirty?"

"Hey, you bring the connotations. Have fun."

"I thought you wanted me to work."

"If you loosen up a little bit, the work will come easier."

"I'm going to be late. Lani hates it when people are late."

"Then by all means, don't be late." He hangs up without saying goodbye.

I fiddle with my hair for another pointless second since it looks exactly the same as it did before I messed with it. I grab my wallet and Lani's sketchbook and head out the door.

* * *

Olio e Limone was miles out of our budget in college. It would have been out of my budget until only a couple of years ago, when the Reed and Lucy books started selling surprisingly well for a children's series. After being a poor college student, then a poor grad student, and then a poor aspiring author, to be able to afford an upscale Italian place feels like a small victory.

Lani's already sitting at a table in a corner, looking at her phone, a glass of wine in front of her. She's always been more sophisticated than me, but she looks like a freaking super-model, still wearing the outfit she had on before, her long fingers tapping swiftly across the phone's screen. She looks like a woman. She's nearly thirty-one. I can't do anything about the fact I'm a couple of years younger, but I'm not a kid anymore. I'll always be a bit untidy, but at least I can afford to buy her dinner.

I'm not late, but I'm not early.

"Hey," I say, sliding into the seat across from her. I place her sketchbook down on the table. A server shows up, saving me from having to decide if I should try to hug her or something. I have no idea how she'd react if I tried to touch her.

Her eyes flick from her phone to her sketchbook, and then up at me. "I completely forgot about this. How did you—"

"The guy from the café asked me to give it to you."

"Jayson? Why?"

"You said we were friends."

She takes the book and slips it into her oversized shoulder bag. "So I did."

I order a beer and we busy ourselves looking at the menu for a few minutes, making small talk about my rental apartment and whether we want to split an appetizer. In the end, we order different everything and when the server has gone, a silence descends.

"So." She tucks some hair behind her ear.

"So."

"Are you seeing someone?" she asks bluntly, but in a rush, as if she had to gear herself up to say it.

I smile nervously. "What do you mean?"

"Isn't that the traditional thing? Estranged spouses thrown back together because one of them needs to get a divorce in order to marry someone else?"

"I don't think there's much traditional about that scenario," I say dryly. "But no, I'm not seeing anyone, and I'm definitely not getting married."

"Oh." Some of the tension seems to go out of her shoulders.

"What about you? Seeing anyone?"

"I see a lot of people," she says flatly.

I shift in my chair, the implication making me itchy. Of course I have no right to an opinion. But if that makes her happy, I won't make a big deal out of it.

"But no one special," I say. Quality is more important than quantity in this area.

She shakes her head, and I'm oddly relieved.

"So we've established we're basically free agents, except for the whole legally married part," she says.

"Yep." This is such a surreal conversation, but what should I have expected? Our entire relationship for the past six years has been surreal.

"Why haven't you asked for a divorce?"

Fuck me. Always with the bluntness. We're falling back into our old pattern: Lani confronts me and I challenge her right back. "Why haven't you?"

CHAPTER 4
LANI

I normally embody the mellowness of both my home state and my adopted one, but since Reed sat down I've been on edge, feeling like an eight ball bouncing hard between pockets. On one hand, I'm having dinner with a stranger, a solid slab of a man who bears only a passing resemblance to The Boy. And on the other, I travel six years in the past with every one of Reed's smiles, with the very sound of his voice. Some things haven't changed at all.

When he asks me why I've never asked for a divorce, it takes me right back to the thick of our relationship. As hard as I push, he doesn't roll over—he pushes me back. If we were school kids, we'd compete to see who could push the other higher, faster, harder on the swing set. If we'd stayed together, maybe we would have kept pushing each other toward success. Or maybe we'd have succeeded in pushing each other right out of our lives.

The real reason I never called an attorney to see how complicated a divorce could be for a quickie Reno marriage is too complicated to encapsulate in a pithy, biting comeback. The truth is, I loved Reed so much, and being his wife was the last real link I had to him. Since no one else was vying for the position, it didn't seem like much harm to keep the connection there.

I've gotten really good at lying by omission. Instead of acknowledging anything so messy as the feelings we may or may not still have for each other, I deflect. "I've been too busy, I suppose. I'm a partner in a design firm."

"Winesap Design, right? Your business seems to be doing really well."

I'm surprised he's heard of it. "We've doubled our growth every quarter for a year. Of course, that's not sustainable without dramatically ramping up our scale, but it bodes well."

"You're crushing it," he says admiringly.

It's not like I'm not willing to take credit for my work, but I shift in my seat, uncomfortable with the naked praise. "Nicole's a bit of a mad genius, but she lets me do my thing, which I appreciate. We've made some good decisions. Once we got into licensing designs, the real money started coming in. The retail side isn't doing badly, either. We might open a satellite location in Ojai."

"That's awesome. You're a business prodigy."

"Not really. I work hard." Sixty-plus-hour weeks aren't unheard of, but the effort has paid off, both with the business growth and my own personal renumeration.

"But you've got an instinct, a head for it. Not like me. If I didn't have Kingston, I'd probably be making a dime per book."

"Kingston—your agent, right?" I remember the name from our collision in the café, and from the dedication of one of the Reed and Lucy books.

"My agent, and a friend."

"Speaking from experience, creative people need to surround themselves with a reliable team if they're going to make any money from their work." Nicole's not stupid, but her eyes glaze over when I start talking about cash flow and retail margins, while those things excite me. We complement each other.

"I'll drink to that," he says, raising his glass of lager.

I clink my glass against his, remembering another toast in another lifetime as I do so. We stood in front of a Reno justice of the peace and swore 'til death do us part, then we celebrated with a buffet dinner—overcooked steak and too-sweet champagne.

"To us," Reed had said, cheeks red.

"To us," I had echoed, happy despite being completely terrified of what we'd done, petrified to tell my friends or my mom that we'd eloped. A week later it became a moot point when he left for Iowa. And I did not.

"So you're on a book tour. That sounds pretty big-time."

"It's to promote the latest release, *Reed and Lucy Go to the Movies*."

I've had it on pre-order since June. "Kids' books, right?" I am such a liar.

"You haven't—" He stops and sighs. "Not that you would. You aren't the target audience, obviously."

"But you're clearly doing well if you're on a book tour."

"We got traction with the second title. Since then, it's been a release about every six months. I have one more on my contract, but I'm having trouble with this next book."

"Writer's block?"

"You could call it that. I'm a little burned out. I'm supposed to be refilling the well and other creativity-related metaphors while I promote the new release. I'm here for a few days, then down to Los Angeles. I have some appearances back in New York later this month."

Right, this is a business trip. His life is on the other side of the country. "You always wanted to live in the big city. I'm glad that worked out for you."

He coughs. "Yes. Well." Before he can say more, the server brings out our food.

I take a bite of my carbonara. It's creamy and tender, but I'd trade the whole plate to know what to say to fill the silence.

Reed pushes his penne around his plate. "Your mom—how's she doing?"

I seize on the topic. "She's really good. Still working at the county public works department. She comes and visits me a couple of times a year, but I'm due for a visit." Mom and Reed always got along when she came to Santa Barbara, but the two of us never flew out there together like we talked about doing one day.

"When was the last time you went back?"

"Her fiftieth was last year, so I went for the party her sisters threw for her. What about you? How's your family?"

The open expression on his face fades. "Oh, you know them."

Actually, I don't. I've never met anyone Reed is related to. He's got an older brother and a younger sister and two living parents who are still married to each other, and yet he's been the closest thing to an orphan since I've known him. His parents wanted him to stay at home, go to State, work in his dad's construction business. He wanted to be a writer. He got into UCSB, took all the writing classes he could. But they refused to support him, financially or any other way. I didn't think his parents could really care that much about what job he had, but I know better than anyone how stubborn Reed is. He must have gotten that trait from somewhere.

"They wouldn't care if I got a seven-figure advance or won the Pulitzer Prize. They think I should have gone to work for Bennet Construction and been happy to do it."

"So you haven't been to visit?" Sacramento is a seven-hour drive from here. It's not inconceivable that he'd go see his family even if he didn't come to see me on the same trip.

"Nah. Josh has a kid, so he texts me pictures from time to time. But Mom and Dad don't want to see me, I guess. Or I don't want to see them."

"That's rough. I would have thought after all this time, after hitting the bestseller lists and getting name-dropped by Michelle Obama."

His expression changes to one of amusement. "You know about that?"

Busted. The former first lady put the first Reed and Lucy book on some year-end best list the Christmas before last. "Uh, yeah, well. I hear things from time to time."

"You follow publishing news as part of your job?" he asks, smiling.

"Not really. I, uh, might have seen your Instagram feed once or twice." I really hope I'm not blushing. It feels like I'm blushing. Shit.

His eyebrows rise. "But you don't have an Instagram."

I cock my head to the side. "How do you know that?"

Now he's the one blushing. "Um."

I laugh. "Okay, so we're both guilty of a little cyberstalking."

"You got me. I look at the Winesap Design account sometimes. Neat stuff."

"That's all Nicole."

"You're no slouch, either. You obviously still draw." He nods toward my bag with the sketchbook inside. "Could I see sometime?"

I freeze. None of my friends knows that once upon a time I fantasized about being an art major before I came to my senses. But Reed always professed to like my work, encouraged me to doodle and sketch and in general waste my time.

After he left, I didn't stop. And now he's back, temporarily. This is a time-out. I can share this with him because he's leaving again in a few days.

"You didn't look?"

"I know better."

Reed's an artist, too. He always wanted to be a writer, but his drawings are incredible. He's got enough sense to ask for permission before checking out someone's private work.

I pull the book out of my bag, flip through a few pages and hold up a still life I've been working on. I rushed out of Wild Child today before I could finish it, so the edges are blurry and undefined, and there's no background, but I'm pretty happy with it so far. "I've been doing a lot of studies of shells lately. Kind of trite."

He takes the book from me gingerly, studies the page. "This is amazing. Are you going to turn this into a vector for a print or something?"

"What?"

"It seems like it would go really well with those coral block prints I saw on the Winesap Design feed a little while ago."

"Huh." It hadn't occurred to me that I'd been unconsciously playing off of Nicole's coral motifs, but now that he's said it, I can't unsee it. She and I have very different styles. Nicole is all about bold lines and colors. I have a more spare approach, with feathery lines and sometimes only the suggestion of a shape, yet in general I'm much more representational while Nicole loves patterns and turning nature into something almost pop-art-inspired.

"You haven't shown this to Nicole, have you?" There's no judgment in his tone, but I bristle anyway.

"No. She's creative, I'm business."

"But it's not like you can't throw out an idea once in a while, right? If she doesn't like it, she'll tell you."

Exactly. If I don't show her, then I never have to find out if she likes it or not.

We pass the rest of the meal making boring small talk more suited to business acquaintances than exes. It's torture, and I'm annoyed with myself by the end of it that I've let it drag on this long.

We tacitly agree to skip dessert. Reed yawns and I remember he's on East Coast time. I move to grab the check. I never let a guy pay for me. Ever. But Reed glares at me and slides the folder out from under my fingers.

"I've got it."

"You're the guest. Let me."

"Lani. I can pay for dinner."

"I know you—" I catch sight of his expression, which is both insistent and vaguely embarrassed, and I remember that neither of us could have afforded a place like this six years ago. I nod and he takes out his wallet. I pretend to be busy with my phone while he pays.

"You want to get a nightcap or something?"

"Nightcap? Are we in the Roaring Twenties?"

He smiles. "I don't know how roaring they are, but it is actually the twenties."

He's got me there. I pretend to be annoyed. "You know what I mean."

"Well, do you want to get a drink? Is that dive where we used to play trivia still open?"

If only it were that simple and we could go back to where we used to drink cheap beer on trivia night and laugh hysterically before stumbling back to our crummy student housing and having enthusiastic early-twentysomething sex. But those days are long gone.

"No. They closed a couple years ago. And you look tired. Come on, I'll give you a ride."

"I can walk."

Why does everything with us have to be a negotiation?

"It's not a problem. I'm parked right around the corner."

Maybe he realizes he doesn't have to fight me on every little thing either because he says okay.

We walk to my car and even in my heels I feel him towering over me. "Jesus Christ, Reed, did you get taller?"

"Um, yeah. Near my apartment in Iowa there was a park with one of those DIY training circuits. I'd go there and work out every day—procrastinating by exercising, basically. That and good old-fashioned Midwestern food bulked me up some, and I think I grew an inch or two that first year. One of my roommates at the moment in Queens is a personal trainer, so he gets me into his gym for free."

"Queens? Roommates?"

"Yes."

Ever since the day I passed a bookstore window and glimpsed *Reed and Lucy Go to the Beach*, written and illustrated by Reed Bennet, prominently displayed, I've been imagining him living in some hip Brooklyn brownstone while the royalty checks pile up. But really, I have no idea what his life is like.

In fact, I don't know Reed at all. I was madly in love with The Boy, but that Reed doesn't exist anymore. He left for Iowa and might as well have died there. I can finally mourn him and move on. For the first time in six years, I have a chance to live my life outside of the shadow of being left by the love of my life. And maybe as part of that, Reed and I can start to be friends again. Or at least get some real closure. I've missed him so much. It would be nice not to have to miss him anymore.

I shiver, even though the night is perfectly warm, and unlock my car with the heavy metal key.

Reed is gawking at my car. "This is what you drive?"

I grin, gratified. "Yep. She's my baby."

"Damn. You always wanted one."

I drive an orange 1969 BMW 2002. I worked closely with the shop to get her spruced up to my specifications. She's the perfect beach-town car, easy to park, zips through traffic with the four-speed manual transmission, and the iconic boxy shape stands out in any parking lot, saving me a lot of time trying to remember where I parked. "I had to put some money into her, had air conditioning put in, but it was so worth it."

"I love it."

"Her name is Makani."

"I love *her*," Reed says, corrected.

My heart apparently can't parse that he's talking about an inanimate object and not me, because it stutters a little bit.

We fasten the heavy belts, and I tune the old-fashioned radio to something modern.

"Didn't you tell me your dad had one of these?"

I have to switch lanes, otherwise I'd be staring at Reed in surprise. "You remember that?"

"Of course I do."

That's a sentiment I'm not touching with a ten-foot pole. Instead of going into the Freudian implications of buying the same vintage model my absentee father used to squire me around the island in, I'm about to ask Reed for directions to his place, but then I get an idea.

"I know you're tired, but can I show you something real quick?"

"Sure."

I hook a left and we start climbing into the foothills. Nicole and Ricky's house isn't terribly far from here, but they're closer to the Mission, and where I'm going is nearer to the flower farms on Route 92. The lots are smaller, the houses older. Our destination is a cul-de-sac. A two-story, cookie-cutter Craftsman sits at the end. It needs a little bit of work, like Makani did when I bought her, but I don't mind. I see the potential in undervalued things. I like to take something that needs a little TLC and put my stamp on it.

The Craftsman's wrap-around porch has a couple of temporary two-by-fours propping up some of the beams, and the stone walkway to the front door is half-missing. Weeds are taking over the front yard. To me, it's beautiful.

I whisper as I share my secret. "I have an offer in on this house."

Reed stares at it, and I wonder what he sees. Does he see all the things that need fixing? Does he see something that's going to take too much work, too much effort? Or does he see what I do? A place that could be a real home, in a way that all the crummy student housing we lived in together, or even the boring if nice apartment I live in now, could never be?

I'm waiting for a verdict from someone whose opinion twenty-four hours ago I would have said didn't matter in the slightest, but I still hold my breath until he turns back to me and says, "It's perfect, Lani."

CHAPTER 5

REED

Lani drives back downtown slowly after asking for the address of my rental. I don't say much. I'm thinking about the house she just showed me, her voice hesitant but filled with unmistakable pride. Does she realize what that house looks like? Does she realize what it means?

"Why that house, Lani?" Maybe if she tells me it's because she's getting a great deal or it's sitting on oil I'll understand and I won't be tempted into thinking things that can't be true.

"I've never lived in a house. In Kauai we lived in apartments, the dorms in college, that shitty rental we had when I was doing my MBA."

I nod. It was pretty shitty—a one-bedroom apartment in Isla Vista that had been beat to hell by the previous occupants and was being let for next to nothing, which is what the two of us could afford.

"Now I'm in a nice place, but I've always wanted someplace where I didn't have someone under me or above me or sharing a wall. I started looking about a year ago, when the business started turning a profit.

"My Realtor, Beverly, hates me. She must have shown me three dozen properties before this one. But the second I saw it, I wanted it. Isn't that absurd? Same with the car. I combed through listings for months and then this popped up and I knew it was the one."

"But what about it did you like?" I press, wanting to know if she's made the same connection I have, the connection to a similar house in the hills that we used to drive by together and spin wishes about back when our daydreams were tangled up in each other and the future we thought we'd be sharing.

"I don't know," she says. It doesn't seem like she's putting me off or hiding anything. "It felt familiar, I guess. Like it was waiting for me."

I smile. Familiar. Yes, I get that. But does she? "Well, I love it."

"Thanks. I'm waiting to hear back on my offer, but Beverly says I'll probably be waiting until Monday."

"Suspenseful."

"Yeah." She sighs.

"So what are you going to do to pass the time?" I ask.

Lani frowns. "Why?"

"I thought maybe we could hang out more. I don't have any plans. I don't even know if any of our friends are still around this area. Amber? Miguel?"

"Miguel moved to Oakland ages ago. Amber…I don't know. We lost touch. I haven't kept up with a lot of those people."

"Oh. But you've got friends, right?" I don't like the idea of her without friends.

"I'm pretty tight with Nicole and her crew. Ophelia lives here in town. Rosie's not far, in Ventura, and Kate lives in L.A., but she's up here all the time, though she and her boyfriend are visiting New York right now."

"So maybe we could do breakfast or brunch or something tomorrow?"

She turns onto my street and parks, shutting the engine off.

The cabin is flooded with silence. I didn't realize how loud the car was until now.

She shifts to face me. "What are we doing here, Reed?"

I know what she's asking, and I don't have a good answer for her. All I know is that I don't want this to be it. A polite dinner between people who used to mean something to each other and then we go our separate ways, this time maybe forever. I have to put some of my cards on the table.

"I know I didn't tell you I was coming so I totally understand if you don't have time for me. And you've got this whole incredible life here—your job is so impressive, and you're kicking ass at it. You're buying a house and you have the fucking coolest car in the world. I'm awed by you, Lani, but I'm not surprised. You've always been amazing. I thought, well, it's been so long I thought I wouldn't need this anymore."

"This what?"

"This." I gesture between us. "Us. Together."

"Together?"

"Not together, together, just together, like in the same place."

"You should ask for your money back from your MFA program. I have no idea what you're talking about." She's trying to sound cool and unaffected, but I know better.

"Yes, you do." I lean over, erasing years of space between us, and kiss her lightly on the mouth. It's familiar and strange and everything I've been feeling since I laid eyes on her in the coffee shop in one perfectly imperfect moment.

She jerks away from me, her mouth sealed into the shape of a kiss, somehow provocative and disapproving at the same time.

"It might be a bad idea…" I trail off when I realize I don't know how to finish the sentiment.

"It's definitely a bad idea."

"You don't even know what I'm going to say."

"It doesn't matter. It's a bad idea."

"You used to like my ideas."

"I used to like you," she retorts.

"You don't like me anymore?"

"I don't know you anymore."

I think about the last few years and how sometimes I feel like I've become a stranger to myself. "I know the feeling."

She furrows her forehead in response.

"Anyway, the probably, definitely bad idea is for you to come inside with me. You could get to know me again. You might like me again. I for sure want to get to know you."

"Know me, like in the biblical sense?" She's rightly suspicious, considering I just kissed her. Chastely, but still.

"Well, yeah, obviously. I'm a breathing human and you're insanely attractive. But I'd settle for friends."

"Can exes be friends?"

"Are we exes? We're still married," I remind her, even though every time it comes up I'm in suspense over whether she's going to take the opportunity to ask for that particular technicality to be severed.

She doesn't say anything, traces the leatherwork of the steering wheel with her elegant fingers with their hard red tips, sexy and contemplative at the same time.

When she starts talking, she speaks slowly, as if choosing her words carefully. "I'm not going to lie and say it's not a little bit nice to see you again. And since you aren't here for very long, I guess there's no harm in hanging out more. But I'm not coming inside. Jesus. Disaster."

She scrunches up her face and I try to guess what she's thinking. Disaster because she's not attracted to me anymore? Or disaster because she thinks we might actually like it if we revisited that aspect of our relationship?

"Brunch seems safe, though."

"Brunch. Sure." I'll take it. "Have any recommendations?"

"Dawn Patrol's good. You can walk there. It'll be packed so be prepared to wait in line. Ten?"

"Ten it is."

"Text me if your plans change. I don't want to be waiting there if you oversleep," she says sternly.

I grin. Her bossy voice really does it for me. "Will do."

"You have my number?"

"Is it the same one?"

"Yes."

"Then I've got it."

"What about you? Same number?"

"No. I've got a 646. I'll text you so you have it." I get out of the car before she can change her mind. "Thanks for the ride."

"Thanks for dinner."

I give her a wave as she starts up the 2002, rattling windows as she accelerates down the quiet residential street. I'm strangely buoyant as I head inside and straight for my sketch-book. I take a few minutes to roughly sketch Lani's house-to-be. Then I turn the page and do a quick sketch of her face in a few lines. The wide nose and beauty mark and the shape of her lips after I kissed them. I haven't drawn this freely in a while, and it feels good.

I don't really believe in muses. Creative work boils down to planting yourself in front of a computer or a drawing board or an easel and getting to work, grinding it out, making a lot of mistakes and a lot of garbage until you do it enough times that eventually you start making it better.

Yet there's something about being happy for the first time in a long time that makes the work flow a little easier, and I'm not too stupid to not take advantage when it's flowing.

I sketch until my yawns become distracting. It's way late New York time. I dig out my phone and text Lani before I turn in.

This is me. Reed Bennet. Your husband. Ha ha.

Sorry. I'm jet lagged. Now you have my number.

Go to sleep, Reed

Just about to. See you tomorrow.

See you then

I fall asleep with my phone in the palm of my hand.

CHAPTER 6

LANI

I rarely dress as elaborately on the weekends as I do when I'm going into the office, so Saturday morning I put on high-waisted jeans, a plain black boatneck tee that always makes me feel vaguely French, flip-flops, and the chunky amethyst bracelet I bought myself when Nicole and I signed our partnership contract. I wear it when I need a reminder of my own strength and badassness. I top it off with a giant floppy straw hat.

I'm going to need all of my strength to get through another meal with Reed.

I had just finished telling myself that I couldn't be interested in someone I haven't interacted with in half a dozen years, whose life is a mystery to me, when he kissed me, and all my good intentions of being friends and getting closure got mixed up in the pressure of his lips on mine and the scent of him, achingly familiar as ever.

When I realize I'm pressing my fingers to my lips as I relive the short, almost friendly kiss, I shake myself. I'm going to have to hustle to make our prearranged meeting on time. That's what I'm calling it: a prearranged meeting. Not a date. You can't date someone you're married to, right?

My phone pings and I'm certain it's Reed texting me to tell me he's not coming, that he's actually a few states away and I'm never going to see him again. That would be par for the course.

But it's not Reed and I don't have time to analyze my mix of relief and disappointment.

OPHELIA

> Jamie & I are at the farmers market. You coming?

I forgot I'd told her I'd be there. Damn Reed and his spontaneously blowing up my weekend, even if the farmers market isn't exactly a can't-miss event. Ophelia is sweet to include me.

> I can't after all, but thanks!

> Don't tell me Nicole has you working on the weekend?

> No, I'm off today, just have a lot to do

> You want me to pick up some greens for you?

> A bunch of chard & a bunch of kale would not be refused

> You got it. I'll drop them off later

> Thx xoxo

It's a little far to walk to Dawn Patrol, so I fire up Makani and park in a lot behind the eatery. In Santa Barbara, your parking budget rivals your gas budget.

As anticipated, there's a line outside, and Reed's already in it. He's wearing the same boots and jeans he was wearing last night, with a fresh shirt that proclaims "Reading Is Fundamental." What a dork. I fight to keep the smile off my face as I walk up to him.

"Good morning."

"Hey!" He lights up when he spots me, and pulls me into an unselfconscious hug, which I return automatically and totally do not overthink. I carefully step out of the embrace after an appropriate amount of time and move a good two feet away from him. "Everything here looks amazeballs. I'm starving."

"Sleep okay?"

"I stayed up late working, but I slept till nine, so I guess I'm on California time now."

"Going to be hard to adjust when you go back."

He ignores that and asks, "So what's good here?"

We talk about the menu and when we reach the counter we order way too much food. I laugh when he adds a side of bacon on top of everything else.

"This is my breakfast and lunch," he explains.

"Whatever. I hope you have a fridge at your place for the leftovers."

"Won't need one," he predicts.

It's too beautiful a day not to sit outside, so we hover on the patio until a table opens up. Reed seems looser than last night, more relaxed, more like The Boy as he absently turns the strap on his wrist and tips his face up to the sun with his eyes closed. He'll be adding to the smattering of freckles on his cheeks if he's not careful.

Not my problem, I remind myself. Even if we're in this strange Bermuda Triangle of friendship, sexual tension, and regret, I promised him we'd hang out, and that's what we're going to do.

"So tell me everything," he says as we settle across from each other. His long legs stretch out beneath the table until his feet cross nearly under my chair. I seriously can't get over how much bigger he is than the twenty-two-year-old I married. I fleetingly wonder if he's grown in other places, then chide myself. Is that even possible? Whatever. I intentionally do not think about his dick as I suck on the straw of my smoothie.

"Everything?" I ask to stall until my brain crawls out of the gutter.

"Everything I missed."

My mind skitters over the long months right after he'd left, when I'd been mired in a bog of emotions, cycling through anger, heartbreak, sadness, and back to anger again, until focusing on finishing my MBA was the only thing that kept me from breaking down completely. Things eventually got better, and once I met Nicole and we started Winesap Design, things got better than better. But he doesn't want to hear about all that.

"Um. You already know about work. Mom. My car. There's not much else to tell."

"Tell me about Nicole. Can I meet her?"

I refrain from bursting out laughing and saying absolutely not. Instead, I have a ready-made excuse. "She and her husband are out of town."

"Maybe next week?"

"Maybe." Reed meeting Nicole would make all of this more real, and way more complicated. "I'm not sure how I would explain you, honestly."

"What do you mean?"

"I guess I could say you're an old friend visiting from out of town."

Reed's easy smile vanishes. "Wait. You've never told her about me?"

"I've never told any of them about you." Why would I tell my friends about the biggest mistake I ever made and give them yet another reason to look at me differently?

"Who's them?"

"The Never a Brides."

The arrival of our various plates of food interrupts his response.

Reed eats a strip of bacon. "Who are the Never a Brides?"

I probably shouldn't have thrown them out there like that, but again, Reed isn't part of our circle, and he never will be. What's the harm in sharing our pact?

"The Never a Brides are—were—Nicole's bridesmaids. We bonded over trying to survive Hurricane Nicole when she was planning her wedding to Ricky. She's incredible. She had enough energy to plan a wedding for several hundred people, keep churning out designs for the business, *and* bug us all about our love lives. We agreed to stick together because we were all content to be single."

I bark out a laugh. "Unfortunately, Nicole didn't have to lift a finger and the other three girls bailed on our little agreement. I'm the only one left."

"They became brides?" Somehow Reed has depleted half the bacon and a third of his breakfast burrito before I've even touched my meal.

"Well, technically none of them are married. But Rosie and Gus bought a house. Ophelia and Jamie are moving in together, too. Kate and Oliver—it's complicated, they just got together, but they're having a baby in a few months." Each of my friends found happiness with people who lift them up, make them happy in the day to day, and who fit into their lives like they were always meant to be there. I never envied them because I knew what it felt like to have that—and then to have it taken away.

Reed sets down his coffee. "So let me get this straight. You and your friends formed a never-getting-married pact, and they actually all found partners but aren't married, while you are single and yet the only married one among them?"

I swallow my first bite of eggs to answer. "Uh. Yeah."

"And they don't know you're married?"

"Correct."

He laughs, long and loud. "This is unbelievable. Truth is stranger than fiction, once again. Babe, you've got to tell them."

"Why? It's not like we're really married."

He winces and I regret putting it like that. He's well aware of the situation.

"I'm only saying you shouldn't lie to people you care about."

My stomach lurches. "I didn't lie. I said I didn't want to get married. I just didn't say the reason for that was because I already am."

He scoffs. "That's a technicality and you know it. I bet you don't tell any of the guys you sleep with you're married, either."

There it is: for every inch I give him, Reed pushes me two inches further. "What does that have to do with anything? And what do you know about it?"

"I don't." He puts his hands up in surrender. "So can I meet them?"

"The Never a Brides?"

"Why not? I'd like to meet your friends."

"I'm not sure that's a good idea." None of this has been a good idea, no matter how hard I try to justify it to myself. "But I'm open to it." I do feel bad that I haven't been entirely honest with the girls. "But under no circumstances can you tell them we happen to be married to each other."

His lips thin out in judgment. "If that's what you want."

"Especially Nicole." I'd never hear the end of it, like, literally never, if she knew I was already married. She'd probably try to arrange couples counseling or something to see if we could make another go of it. Which is ridiculous.

"I get it," Reed says impatiently. The judgmental look stays, and great, now I feel doubly guilty.

"If she knows we eloped and stayed married, she's going to think it's because we still have feelings for each other and her not-so-latent matchmaker gene will flip on like a light switch.

She can't even know that we're exes. I'll tell her you're my friend from college who's in town for a book tour."

"I am your friend from college who's in town for a book tour." His tone is dry but his grumpy expression lifts a little, and I instantly feel better.

I stick my tongue out at him. "You know what I mean."

"I'm not sure I want to meet her anymore. I mean, she sounds kind of intense."

Defensiveness kicks in. "I know I give her a hard time, but Nicole is really the best. She's super smart, and she's brilliant when it comes to design. She's not afraid to iterate. She tries something new and then moves on if it doesn't pan out. It's a very fast-paced way to work, but it really gets us to what sells faster."

"You're too humble," Reed says, his mood shifting again.

"Huh?"

"Giving her so much credit when it's obvious you're the one who's made the whole operation viable."

I shake my head. "It's a team effort."

He smiles and offers me some bacon. "I'm sure Nicole would agree with me, if I ever get the chance to ask her."

I'm desperate to get onto a different subject and jump on the first one that passes through my brain. "So what about you? What about ladies? You said there wasn't anyone special, but you probably have plenty of offers. You know, sexy librarians and single moms. Spill."

He shakes his head. "You don't want to hear about that."

Probably not. "Tell me anyway." Hearing about his conquests will at least remind me that while we might be getting to know each other again, this relationship isn't heading anywhere but Friendsville.

CHAPTER 7
REED

This conversation has been a wild ride and I'm hanging on for dear life. Thank goodness the bacon is keeping me grounded in deliciousness.

But when Lani asks about my conquests, I don't know what to say. She can't honestly want to hear details, but she seems determined.

"Okay, well. In Iowa, there was Michaela. She was in the program with me. Super smart, extraordinary writer. Still in love with her ex, so, you know, we had a lot in common." I sneak a glance at Lani, who is eating her eggs with laser focus.

I don't let myself dwell on the cocktail of defiance, guilt, and depression that led me to start up with Michaela. Nearly a year after I arrived, I had the painful realization that mutual friends-with-benefits was the best I could hope for, since Lani was clearly not going to be showing up at my doorstep to tell me she missed me and wanted me back. My pride was damaged; becoming a writer, the goal that led me to Iowa in the first place, was the only thing I had left.

"After I finished the program and moved to New York, I knocked around for a while, and eventually I met Erin. Not exactly a sexy librarian, but close enough. She's an assistant editor at one of the big publishing houses."

Lani looks up, pushes her plate away. "What was wrong with her?"

"What do you mean?"

"You guys broke up for a reason, right?"

"Oh, she dumped me for a contracts attorney. They recently got engaged."

"Sorry," she says mildly.

"It's fine." And it really is. I spent a lot of time with Michaela and Erin, but that's all it was, a way to pass the time. I was never in love with them. Lani, however, was never far from my thoughts, no matter how far I got from her.

Now she's right here in front of me and for some reason I'm talking about other women. *Way to go, Reed.*

"And then?" Lani says.

"And then what?"

"Who else?"

"No one else."

Lani's eyes open comically wide. "You've only slept with two people since—"

I laugh at her obvious shock. "Yes."

"Wow. That's—"

"Pathetic?" I don't even want to know what her number is. Thinking about her with other guys is something I spend a lot of energy pointedly *not* doing.

"I was going to say in character. You're a romantic, Reed. You don't do casual, right? Those women were probably really good for you. I'm glad you had them." Surprisingly, she actually sounds like she means it.

They were good for me. They both turned out to be good friends in the end. "Thanks. That's very mature."

She sticks her tongue out at me in response and I laugh again. I haven't laughed this much in a long time.

"It's been a while for you, then?" she says, toying with the straw of her half-drunk smoothie.

"Been a while?" I swallow the last bite of my burrito and show off my clean plate. "See, no leftovers."

"Now I see how you managed to grow so much. Been a while since you had sex, I mean."

"Jesus. Okay, yeah. Thanks for rubbing it in."

"I wonder if that's why you have writer's block. You know, when you're backed up in other areas." She smiles slyly.

"I take back what I said about your maturity level. You still have a dirty mind." Lani's ability to turn the most innocent remark into innuendo always surprised and delighted me.

"Hey, pretty much everyone thinks about sex most of the time. I'm just honest about it."

She has a smug expression on her face, and I have the strongest urge to kiss it off of her. And not because it's been a while.

"What's on tap for the rest of the weekend?" Lani asks briskly, giving me whiplash. "You should probably do some work on your book, right?"

"I should. My draft is due to Kingston when I get back, but you know me, I like to procrastinate."

"I remember you used to wait until the day your papers were due and pull fifteen pages out of thin air."

"Not out of thin air. Out of my highly advanced brain," I say.

She laughs merrily. "Oh, I know all about your brain. Should I drop you at your place or—"

"Let's not ruin this beautiful day with work. What do you normally do on the weekend?"

"You know, the typical. Most Saturdays at this time I'm at the farmers market."

We used to go together sometimes and stare at all the beautiful local produce we couldn't afford, then buy bruised fruit at half price.

But the successful, put-together woman sitting across from me can afford whatever she wants now. She's even buying an entire house. She's always been way too good for me, and I wonder what she sees when she looks across the table at me. Does she see someone who has got it together, someone who deserves the time of day from her? Or does she see the boy from the past who nearly broke from missing her so badly, who struggled to make rent every single month for years, who regrets being so wrapped up in his own stupid dreams that he lost the best thing that ever happened to him?

It's confusing to be around her, one foot in the past, one foot in the present, not even daring to think one minute more into the future.

"Well, if you're going to procrastinate anyway, then I guess you can be useful and help me keep my mind off the offer."

"You haven't heard from your Realtor?"

"Not a whisper."

"By all means, press me into service as a mode of distraction."

"Thanks." She nods assertively. "Let's go back to my place."

CHAPTER 8
LANI

Like every decision I've made since Reed popped back into my life yesterday, I'm second-guessing this one from the moment I make it. Bringing him to my apartment seemed harmless when I'd suggested it, but now that he's in my space, I wonder what I was thinking.

I live alone. I'm a girl. Hence, my girly shit is everywhere, from the nest of hair ties on the kitchen table to the lacy underwear drying over the towel rack in the bathroom. I clear that out hastily, throwing it blindly into my bedroom and shutting the door. There's no reason for him to see that particular room on this particular visit. Or any visit, for that matter.

Reed dwarfs my functional blond wood Scandinavian furniture, and looks like a giant next to my armchair, which isn't technically child's size, but is the smallest, coziest one I could find. I had it reupholstered in dark teal velvet and it's my favorite spot to sit and read or sketch, with the view of the courtyard outside through my balcony's sliding glass door. The courtyard is filled with plumeria and birds of paradise. It reminds me of the apartment building where we lived when I was little—before my dad left and my mom and my sister and I moved to a cheaper, uglier development.

"Want something to drink?" I don't know what I have to offer—I'm not often a hostess. If I bring someone back to my place, we've generally already imbibed at whatever watering hole we met at, and conversation isn't on the menu. When I hang out with my friends, we usually go to Nicole's roomy modern house that was designed for entertaining, or to the beach.

"Sure," Reed says easily, scanning my bookshelf.

I open the fridge and look into it blindly. What am I doing? Why is he here? Why, when I could have taken the exit to end our hanging out, did I skip it and bring him back here? Why, why, why?

"Did you like *Normal People*?" he calls from the living room.

I draw a blank until I realize he's talking about the book. "Oh yeah. It was good. Sad." I grab a can from the shelf, close the door. "Sparkling water okay?"

"Thanks." He abandons the bookshelf and comes toward the kitchen, taking the can from my outstretched hand. Our fingers brush a little, and I shiver. Maybe it's from the cold refrigerator air.

Maybe I'm a shit liar, even to myself.

Maybe I know exactly why I asked him back here.

Maybe he does, too.

The crack of the can opening shakes me out of my internal panic. Just because I got him here doesn't mean I have to do anything.

"So," I start, not sure how I'm going to end the sentence, when a rap sounds sharply on my door. We both glance at it with curiosity. I have no idea who might be knocking on my door, since my packages normally get left downstairs and all my friends—oh. Ophelia.

I open the door to Ophelia, who carries a tote bag with leafy greens spilling over the top.

"Hey, O, thanks." Is it horribly rude to blatantly ignore the man hovering in the background behind me?

"No problem. I was going to leave them at your door, but I'm glad you're here. You should put the kale in the fridge, it already looks a little wilted."

She peers over my shoulder and gives Reed a little wave. "Hi." Her gaze cuts to me, a questioning look on her face.

I squeeze my eyes shut for a second, coming to terms with the inevitable, then open the door wider. "You want to come in and meet a friend?"

O puts on her polite face, the one she uses with strangers. She can take a while to warm up to new people. "Ophelia, this is Reed Bennet. Reed, this is Ophelia, Nicole's cousin."

"Hi, Ophelia," he says, offering her an easier grin than he's ever given me. I fight the urge to frown. Or to walk over and lace my arm through his. He only belongs to me on paper, not in reality. "Really nice to meet a friend of Lani's."

"Reed Bennet?" Her polite face gives way to a startled smile. "The author?"

"That's me," he says, a little bashful, which seems weird.

"Oh my gosh, my students love your books. *I* love your books. They're so witty and insightful. And the drawings—every page is so memorable, with all those tiny details. We're so looking forward to the new one."

Reed looks taken aback by Ophelia's gushing, but before I can explain, she does.

"I'm a librarian at Clinton Elementary. I just had to order a new copy of *Reed and Lucy Go to the Park* because the old one was in tatters from being read so many times. But my favorite is *Reed and Lucy Go to the Library*, for obvious reasons."

My consternation grows as Reed accepts the compliment with a blush on his cheeks. I've never seen Ophelia open up to someone new this fast, and it's disconcerting. Reed's telling her about the new book when Ophelia interrupts him.

"Wait, how do you know Lani? She never told me she knew one of my favorite children's book authors." She looks between the two of us expectantly.

"Um—" I begin.

"Well—" Reed adds helpfully.

"Oh my gosh, you're Lucy!" Ophelia's expression transforms again, this time into incredulity. "I can't believe I never saw it before. But look at you—Lucy even has the same mole on her cheek."

"I prefer to call it a beauty mark," I say, trying to recover some of my equilibrium.

"You must be old friends," Ophelia says. "Did you know each other as kids, like Reed and Lucy?"

"No, we met in college," Reed says, glancing at me. "But it feels like we've known each other forever."

"You went to UCSB, too? I'm an alum, but I must have been after your class. This is amazing, what a small world. I can't believe Lani never said anything." She looks at me, her eyes full of questions.

I wish I had answers for her.

"Well, thanks for bringing the veggies over. I'll Venmo you for them later, okay?"

"Wait, do you live here in town? Do you ever do school visits? I'd love to show you my library sometime. The kids would be over the moon."

"I'm just visiting Santa Barbara right now. But I am going to some schools as part of my book tour for *Reed and Lucy Go to the Movies*. I'm sure I could add one more, if you can squeeze me in this week."

"Anytime! Tell me what works for you."

Before I can stop them, they're exchanging phone numbers and checking their calendars and Reed promises to spend Tuesday morning at Clinton Elementary School.

Ophelia's so jazzed she can barely contain herself. "You

have to let me do something to thank you. You should come out for dinner with us, let me buy you a steak or something."

Reed looks at me. I shrug. I don't have any claims on his time. He's a free agent.

"Oh shoot, I can't do it tonight, but maybe tomorrow. Wait, tomorrow night Jamie's parents are having a barbecue. I was going to invite you, Lani, so you and Reed can both come!"

I don't like how she's lumping us together, consciously or not.

"Who's Jamie?" Reed asks.

"Jamie is Ricky's cousin, and my—" They've been together since February and are planning to move in together when Ophelia's lease is up in a couple of months, but it's still cute to see her hesitate a little bit over the word. "—boyfriend."

"Your cousin married his cousin?"

"We like to keep it in the family. You have to come meet everyone. Ricky and Nicole won't be back from their trip, but I'll see if Rosie and Gus are free to come up."

"I don't know."

Reed talks over me. "We'll be there. What should we bring?"

"*I'll* bring a salad," I say, trying to nip all this "we" business in the bud.

"You don't have to bring anything, but Jamie's family is very into desserts."

"I'll come up with something," he says agreeably.

"This is so exciting. We don't usually have a celebrity at our Sunday family dinners."

"Celebrity?" I resist the urge to laugh. Reed shakes his head, the blush returning. What the hell is up with all the blushing?

"In my world, Reed Bennet is a big deal. Lani, it would be like if some big designer walked into Winesap. Like the founder of Coral & Tusk or something."

"Seriously?" I know his books are big sellers, but I've never thought of Reed himself as a public figure.

"I better go, but I will see you tomorrow night. Lani knows where it is. Bye, Reed." Ophelia lets herself out and I walk over to shut the door behind her. She points a finger at me and in a low voice says, "You have explaining to do. Call me tomorrow."

I nod, resigned. I should have known that keeping any of this a secret would be futile, especially since Reed seems so intent on learning about my life and now ingratiating himself with my friends. I thought he'd be in and out as fast as the trend for driftwood lamp bases, but even though he's only been here two days, he's sticking.

I worry that when he inevitably goes back to New York, back to his real life, an echo of his presence will be left behind like a ghost. Only I won't be able to erase him as easily as stray pencil marks in my sketchbook.

CHAPTER 9
REED

"So that was Ophelia. Great name," I remark after Ophelia is gone. Lani seems annoyed, but I can't tell if she's irritated with me specifically or because she's been foiled in her attempt to keep me isolated from her friends. "This barbecue sounds fun."

"They're probably going to love you." She doesn't sound happy about it. "I guess we should carpool. I'll pick you up at six. Get something good for dessert. They like pie."

"Who doesn't?" I take another tour around Lani's place. It's not huge, but it's bright and open.

She's made a home for herself here, one light years nicer than any place we lived as students, and way better than my Queens hovel. But I can see why she'd want to level up to a house. She'll want to put her stamp on every room, make everything just so, from the paint to the drawer pulls.

The big wall behind the sofa in this room is completely covered in bookshelves; she has a large, eclectic collection, cookbooks and paperback novels, coffee table books on design, and—

Wait. I spy a familiar set of spines on the farthest, highest shelf, partially hidden by a tiny green succulent in a terra-cotta pot.

Hadn't she said—? But there they are, all five of them. All that's missing is the new release. I turn to where she's sitting in her miniature blue armchair with her bare feet tucked up underneath her. "I thought you hadn't read my books."

She bites her lip and has the gall to look chagrined. "Oh. Well. Technically, I didn't say that. I just let you think it."

I shake my head. She is unbelievable. "I don't remember you being such a liar, Lani. First you lie to your friends about me, and then you lie to me about my books. What the hell?"

"I—look, you're driving me crazy. You show up out of the blue, all tall and...firm—"

Firm? I don't have time to process that particular adjective because she goes on. "And you say things that I don't under-stand and I thought we could maybe be friends or get closure or something, but this is getting confusing."

I have to smile at that. I always could get under her skin. Guess I haven't lost my touch.

"Why are you doing this?" she asks quietly.

"What?" I'm honestly confused.

"Being so nice. Wanting to meet my friends and go to barbe-cues and going to Ophelia's school. What are you getting out of it? You'll be back in New York in a few days and you won't see any of these people ever again."

I don't entirely know myself, so I try to put what I do know into words. "I'm...interested. Your friends are interesting. Your life is interesting. You're interesting." She's built up this entire world without me, and I can't help but be curious about it.

Her life may have changed, but her facial expressions haven't. Right now she's looking at me like I'm exasperating her.

"But why? What's the point?"

"The point? I'm curious about the world. I'm a writer. I like to meet new people and have new experiences."

"Oh, so this is all potential material for a new book? *Reed and Lucy Go to a Barbecue?*"

"No. Not exactly." I'm uncomfortably aware that I've been guilty of mining our real-life experiences—hers and mine—for book fodder in the past. Hell, most of the pieces I wrote for my MFA were about lovelorn college boys and their maddening relationships with gorgeous, fiercely independent women.

They say write what you know.

"Do you know how I came up with the idea for Reed and Lucy in the first place?"

"No."

"I wrote you letters. When I was in Iowa. Never sent them, of course. I was supposed to be working on my great American novel and all I wanted to do was talk to you. I was too proud to call you, to tell you how lonely I was. I wrote to you instead, longhand, on paper, like the pretentious fool I was, and in the margins I drew us. I'd draw us doing all the things we liked to do together, going for drives, sketching together, going to the beach and exploring the tide pools. I'd imagine us before all our baggage. That's when I started turning us into characters who were kids."

I can see Lani taking all that in. I hope I'm not making things worse by being candid, but I'm getting tired of holding things back, of having her straight up lie to my face.

"Just friends?" she says.

That's how we started out, after all. "I guess I was envisioning a fictional, innocent time. That's how Lucy came to be."

"I'm not Lucy," she says firmly.

"No, you aren't Lucy. While I was gone, you grew up. You've grown into such a gorgeous, incredibly competent, successful woman. The world bends to your will, Lani. You can have anything, anyone you want." I pause, making sure she's looking at me when I say, "But Lucy is you." Without Lani, Lucy wouldn't exist.

She visibly shakes her shoulders, as if shaking off what I've said. "What about you? Are you still that little kid? The Reed from the books?"

The Reed of the books is a version of me who didn't lose his family, his friends, his love by putting his stupid dream of being a writer above everything else. "No. I grew up, too. I got the dreamer beaten out of me. When I left here, I thought I had everything figured out, but every year since has tied for sucking the most. Iowa was everything I thought I wanted and I was miserable. New York is worse."

"You really hate it that much?"

"I could give you a laundry list of all the things I don't like about New York, but I'll save that for another day."

"Sounds like a great time," she says flippantly. "Remind me to visit."

I'm suddenly overcome by a wave of bitterness and collapse onto the sofa within arm's reach of the blue armchair. I left and Lani thrived. She finished her degree, started an entire company, dated and made new friends, and in general lived her best life, all without me. I struggled and then lucked into success doing something that barely counts as writing. I think up kids' stories and draw pictures to go with them.

"You know I didn't set out to be a children's book author. I was going to be a novelist. I wanted to write a book that Michael Silverblatt would call 'wildly inventive' on *Bookworm*."

She presses her lips together as she tries to hold back a laugh, then snorts a little as she can't quite manage it. "You are such a snob. You don't even know what your books mean to people, do you?"

"Kids love Reed and Lucy because they're silly and funny, not because it's great literature."

"*That's* why you got all blushy when Ophelia was lavishing you with praise. Reed, the world doesn't need more quote-unquote great literature. But thousands of families read and love your stories. You make them smile. You make them love words and language. That's important."

"You really think that?"

"Of course." She reaches out to touch my knee. I hold still, relishing the point of contact between us.

"I love them, too," she says quietly. "Reed and Lucy are the best version of what we used to be. I like knowing you remember the good times."

"I do, Lani."

A silence falls between us, and she shifts away, taking her hand off my knee. We're entering dangerous territory—actual honesty, actual progress made on our becoming something new to each other. But I'm scared that if I push this time, I'll mess up this fragile balance. I swerve to a new topic.

"These pillows are really comfortable."

"Those are from the store."

"I can't wait to check it out."

Lani makes a strangled sound at that, and I look over at her, unable to decode her expression this time.

She straightens her shoulders. "Do you want a ride home, or do you want to call a car?"

Damn. I have no right to monopolize her weekend, but I want to anyway. "What about dinner? I feel like I owe you after brunch. We could order takeout? Watch a movie?" I glance around. She doesn't seem to have a TV, but there's a gleaming silver laptop on the coffee table.

She makes the sound again, like a frustrated cat, and stares at me like I'm nuts. Maybe I am, because it belatedly occurs to me that if I stay and we watch a movie on her laptop, huddled together so we can both see the screen, it will be far too much like the old days. We spent a hundred Saturday nights the exact same way, more often than not making out as the credits rolled, or even before, depending on how good the movie was. We practically invented Netflix and chill.

Doing it now, I don't know if I could handle it. The temptation to kiss her would be overwhelming, and I know if I give in to that impulse, I won't want to stop there.

My thoughts must be playing on my face, because she stands up briskly. "I can't, Reed."

"Okay." I stand up awkwardly, ignoring the way I've grown half-hard just thinking about kissing her. "I'll find my own way home, thanks. See you tomorrow."

"Sure. Six."

"Six it is." I'd torture myself by kissing her goodbye on the cheek, but the semi I'm sporting makes it seem like a safer bet to head straight for the door. "Until then."

I let myself out, and I think I hear her make that strangled cat sound from the other side of the door before I walk stiffly down the hallway to the stairs.

CHAPTER 10
REED

I've gotten my bearings and am walking down a jacaranda-lined avenue, trying to cool off and failing due to the late summer heat when my phone rings. For a second I hope it's Lani, telling me she's changed her mind about dinner, but it's Kingston.

"What?" I answer irritably, even though none of this is his fault. Oh yes, except for all of it. He's the one who encouraged me to come on this trip down memory lane.

"Wow, you need to get laid," he says. His thoughts parallel my own, which doesn't improve my grouchiness.

"Speak for yourself," I mutter.

"As a matter of fact, I had a successful date last night with a very handsome Broadway up-and-comer. And he stayed for breakfast, so fuck you."

"Well, good for you. I got kicked out of Lani's apartment just for thinking lascivious thoughts."

"Ooh, I like it. *Reed and Lucy and the Lascivious Thoughts.*"

"Gross, Kingston. You do realize you're making a sex joke about a children's book?"

"Well, excuse me for being in a good mood. How's the new

book? Are you channeling all your sexual frustration into another bestseller?"

I debate telling him I did get some work done, but he deserves to suffer. "You'll see a draft when I'm done."

"You better be working. But not on an epic novel. I don't want this to be a *Wonder Boys* situation."

I laugh. In one of my favorite movies, Michael Douglas's author character keeps putting off his editor because he doesn't want to tell him his new book has ballooned to over two thousand pages.

"Relax. I've only been working on this book for seven months, not seven years."

"I just want to make sure you have what you need."

"I need you to stop bugging me. By the way, I'm going to another elementary school on Tuesday to do a reading. Can you overnight the librarian there some copies of the new book?"

"I'm not your personal assistant, you know. And when did you book that?"

"Today. The librarian is a friend of Lani's. She's a fan of Reed and Lucy."

"Maybe you should bang her instead."

"She's taken. And I'm not banging anyone."

"My point exactly."

"Look, stop obsessing over my sex life and send out those books."

"Text me the address and it's done."

"Thanks."

I turn right onto State Street and am hit with blast of sun baking the terra-cotta roofs of the Spanish-style shops. The sidewalk is crowded with weekend shoppers, homeless people holding creative, snarky signs, families with ice cream-sticky kids, and leashed dogs of every shape and size.

I don't want to be a tourist in this paradise. I want to be a permanent part of it. I've never felt as home for a day in New York as I do as a hanger-on in Santa Barbara.

It's not because I'm from here. But it's the first—the only—place I ever felt like I belonged. Where I met people who thought it was cool that I liked to read and wanted to be a writer, not lame and weak. Where being good at school was a plus. Where girls dug my vibe. Well, one girl.

Lani got me and seemed to like me for who I was. She didn't care that I reread *The Perks of Being a Wallflower* every year on my birthday, or that I was a little chubby because I'd rather draw and scribble in my notebook than skateboard, or God forbid, play a sport. Is it any wonder that when I found someone who accepted me, who loved me for who I was, I wanted to keep her in my life forever? I thought us being in love was enough.

Getting married seemed to me like the natural extension of our relationship. I didn't know that getting into my top-choice MFA program off the waitlist would change my priorities—or expose the truth that Lani wasn't as in love with me as I thought. Otherwise, she would have come with me, instead of digging in her heels and giving me an unequivocal no. At least, that's what I thought at the time.

Reed-in-the-books and Lucy have the kind of pure, unconditional love that I imagined Lani and I had. But it turned out the limits of Lani's love were closer to home than I thought. She could love me in Santa Barbara. She could love me when my dreams of writing a great novel were just that: dreams. But when it came to actively supporting those dreams, helping me make them a reality and moving to a new place, the love ran out, I guess.

If I move back here, we couldn't pick up where we left off. We're both way too different now. She's sleek and sophisticated. Successful. At heart, I'm still the same chubby, non-athletic reader who'd rather doodle than do almost anything. I haven't written a great novel and maybe I never will.

But one thing is clear. After two days of California sunshine, I'm only going back to New York to pack up my shit.

"Kingston, you there?"

"No, I ran away to sing backup for Adele."

"I'm over New York for good."

"About damn time. You hate it here."

"Was I that obvious?"

"As a traffic light. You think you'll end up back in Santa Barbara?"

"Depends."

"Depends on your girl?"

Yes. "No."

He snorts into the phone. "Whatever. I'm proud of you. You're finally standing up and going after what you want."

"What are you talking about?"

"Ever since I've known you you've always been reacting, doing what other people told you to do. Your MFA advisor said you should go to New York, your girlfriend told you to write a children's book, I told you to sell it as a series, the publisher told you to write three books a year. It's time you figured out what you want."

"I want..."

I don't know what I want. Or rather, I want the same things I wanted six years ago. I want Lani, and to write a great novel, and to show my parents my dreams weren't stupid. I want to be twenty-two and get a second chance not to screw up the best thing I ever had.

Kingston laughs again when I never finish the sentence. "Yeah, I know."

I give my phone the finger even though he can't see me, dodging pedestrians as I make my way toward the beach. "You think you know everything."

"I know what's good for you. And I know you'll be happier there, even if it's not with her."

As much as I don't want to give him the satisfaction, I hum my agreement. "Thanks, Kingston." He might be an insufferable know-it-all, but he has my back, personally and professionally.

"Take care out there," he says, and clicks off.

When I hit the sand, I fold down to my knees and stare over the gray-green Pacific, oblivious to the less contemplative Saturday beachgoers around me. I sit and think for so long it starts to cool down, the sun inching toward the horizon and gilding everything I can see in rose gold. The golden hour. It's so pretty to look at it hurts.

I'm still in love with this place, with the feeling I could belong here, with the dream that it could be my home again.

Maybe I'm still in love with Lani, too.

CHAPTER 11

LANI

* * *

Ophelia is waiting for me outside the landmark Scandinavian bakery when I arrive. She looks Sunday-casual, for her, in a vintage sweater and pleated lavender skirt that would look ridiculous on me but makes her look like the sweet children's librarian she is.

We get seated on the patio and order coffee before I head her off at the pass.

"I should have known you would know who Reed Bennet is."

"He's only one of the hottest names in picture books right now."

"You make him sound like a rock star."

"He basically is, to the five-to-eight-year-old set. How precisely do you know him?"

I don't like lying to her, but since I've been doing it by omission from the day we formed the Never a Bride club, I don't have much choice. They say the best lies are based on the truth. "He's actually my ex."

"I knew it!" she exclaims. "He didn't seem like a recent conquest."

"What?" Conquest? "We met in college, we dated. Then he moved away."

"How long were you together?"

I pretend to think about it, even though the dates are etched on my memory. "About three years."

"Oh wow. I had no idea you—" She breaks off when the server comes with our steaming coffee and a plate of pastries. The look Ophelia gives them is that of a woman in love. She looks at those pastries the way she looks at Jamie. I push the plate closer to her and she takes a chocolate croissant reverentially.

Since her mouth is full and I don't really want to know what she was going to say, I take control of the conversation. "He moved to Iowa to get his MFA and we broke up. We haven't really kept in touch, but when he came back into town for his book tour, he reached out and we've been hanging out a little."

"But you knew about his books, about Reed and Lucy? Have you read them?"

"Yes," I say, a little reluctantly. I don't know why I shouldn't admit it.

"You are totally Lucy," she says. "This is so cool. I'm friends with the character of a children's book. This is like a dream come true for me!"

"I'm not Lucy," I insist pointlessly. "She's just a drawing in a book."

"Who looks exactly like you."

"She's five."

"Come on, don't tell me you didn't see the resemblance."

"I did." I'd been a little weirded out, because seeing Lucy made me realize Reed must have had me on his mind. Unless I was just a jumping-off point, a muse for his creativity, and Lucy had become a different character for him, one that only had a passing resemblance to me. Either way, I could have chosen to get persnickety about it, calling him and angrily demanding to know what gave him the right to use our shared history as fodder for a book.

But I didn't.

Because the story was beautiful. The drawings spoke to me even more than the words. They reminded me of being happy. With Reed. Lucy is a lot of things I don't think I am—kind, patient, wise. But I liked her. And it was kind of like a secret identity, my kids' book alter ego no one knew about except for Reed and me. And even though we didn't talk in real life, it was like he was talking to me through the pages of the book. It was as if we were having a slow-motion, one-sided conversation and I had to wait six months between updates.

So yes, I was conflicted. But in the end, I didn't have the heart to tell him to stop. The world fell in love with Reed and Lucy, like I did, and then I really had no right to take that away from them. I didn't want to.

"Well, consider my mind blown. I got to meet Reed Bennet. We're all alums from the same school. You dated him! He's not how I pictured him. I mean, the book jacket bio includes his self-portrait that makes him look like a grown-up version of Reed from the book. But he's rather...masculine."

My mind turns over the word. "He's grown up a lot since we were together. He used to have baby fat and wear cardigans."

"Hmmm. Well, he's kind of a dish."

"You think?"

"Definitely, very manly but emo, with those heavy boots and leather bracelet. He looks like he listens to a lot of Pearl Jam and reads Vonnegut."

I laugh. "I always thought he was kind of a nerd." It had been one of things that had confused me about him. He liked comics and reading and attended lectures from guest speakers on topics like the philosophical implications of climate change. He also loved Monty Python and his favorite movie was *Groundhog Day*. I liked that he was into a bunch of different things. He was much more interesting than the guys in my circle of friends who were mostly into binge drinking and complaining about their sports teams. And we both liked to draw. That was the main thing we had in common—we'd spend hours sketching together. But he also pushed me. He was the one who encouraged me to apply for an MBA, when my plan had been to get an entry-level job someplace after graduating.

"Hey, nerds are hot, speaking as someone who's in love with one."

"Your nerd is very hot," I reassure her. "Are you sure it's okay to bring Reed to the barbecue tonight?"

"Are you kidding? They're going to be stoked. And Rosie and Gus said they could come. If Kate and Oliver weren't in New York, we could have a little reunion."

"I guess it's been a while since we've all gotten together."

"I never thought I'd say this, but I kind of miss Nicole in wedding-planning mode. She brought us all together. It was nice."

"Don't ever tell her that."

"Oh, don't worry, I won't." Ophelia smiles sunnily. "Too bad Reed lives in New York. I think he'd fit right in with the boys."

It hadn't occurred to me, but he'll probably get along famously with Jamie, an inventor and maker at a kids' science museum, and Gus, who is the director of horticulture at a botanical garden a few miles south. "I don't think he likes New York much. He's a California boy to the bone."

"Maybe he'll come back."

I twitch. After some of his comments, I suspect that might not be out of the realm of possibility. It was easy to ignore the circumstances of our leftover marriage when he was a conti-nent away. But one of these days we're going to have to face facts and actually do the divorce thing. Sentimentality and an aversion to paperwork aren't good enough reasons to keep putting it off.

"Anyway, I have some errands to run, but I'll see you and Reed tonight."

"Okay." I bite my lip. I feel like I should tell her. "O?"

"What is it?"

I can imagine her face when I say the words *I'm married*, and I chicken out. "Never mind."

CHAPTER 12
REED

"What did you do today?" Lani asks me over the growl of Makani's engine as she pulls away from the curb outside my rental. I'm balancing a brown box on my lap, hoping the peach pie I found at a nearby bakery passes muster with our hosts. I glance over my shoulder; an enormous salad bowl covered in some kind of printed waxed fabric sits in the backseat.

"This and that." I'd half-heartedly tried to work, then scrolled nearby apartment listings, only taking a break to go pie shopping. I wanted to call Lani but erred on the side of not wearing out my welcome. "How much salad do you think we're going to eat? That bowl is as big as a swimming pool."

"Trust me, this crowd can eat. I might have gotten a bit carried away, but I don't have many opportunities to cook."

"Why not?"

"Not much fun to cook for one," she says casually.

"You don't cook for your, um, gentleman friends?"

She shakes her head. "Definitely not."

I leave that alone and move on. "You look amazing, by the way."

"Thanks. You look nice."

I'm wearing jeans and a flannel button-down with my boots. I didn't have much choice since I'm limited to what I packed. I look fine. She, on the other hand, looks like a rock star in a floral print jumpsuit, brown high-heeled sandals, and big hoop earrings. Her nails are lacquered in red, while her mouth is covered in a sheen of sheer gloss. I want to kiss her. Would she taste sticky or sweet?

I clear my throat. "Give me the rundown of who-all's going to be at this shindig."

"Ophelia, you met. Jamie's her beau. His parents are hosting: Laura and Rory. Rory is Ricky's dad's brother. And then Rosie, one of the Never a Brides. She's coming with her boyfriend, Gus. There might be a smattering of neighbors, I guess. The Winesap-Kendells are definitely more-the-merrier types."

"Sounds fun."

"It's nice to be included." She turns into a more residential part of town, and the elevation climbs slightly. "I told O you were my ex, by the way."

"But not your husband."

"Stop saying that." She's got her exasperated face on again and I can't help my answering smile.

"Why?"

"Just—okay?"

"So I'm your ex." True enough. "Any single ladies in your crew?"

"They're all taken, thank goodness."

I pretend to be offended. "Hey. Well, how about single guys? There's bound to be a brother or a cousin who's pining for you, right?" I can only imagine how many hearts Lani breaks on a regular basis.

"Ricky's an only child. I did have a fun time with one of his groomsmen, Zack. But I try not to mix business and pleasure."

"Smart," I say with a distinct lack of enthusiasm. I should have known she'd call my bluff.

"We're here. Be good."

"I'm always good," I respond. Lucky for me, she's not looking as I check her out when she leans into the back seat to get out her oversized salad bowl.

Carrying our offerings, we don't bother with the front door to the two-story ranch and instead head for the backyard, where a small group has gathered. The men are clustered around a grill, while I recognize Ophelia on the other side of the patio. She's talking to a dark-haired woman in a red dress.

She sees us and breaks into a smile, crossing over. "Reed, so glad you could make it. Let me take that. Jamie!" A tall, lanky white guy in glasses and a shirt with a chemical equation on the front saunters up. "Jamie, this is Lani's friend Reed, visiting from New York, who happens to be the author of one of the best children's book series of the past few years. Reed, this is Jamie."

Jamie gives Lani a hug and waves to me, then Ophelia and Lani abandon us to put the salad with the rest of the food. Another guy, a little shorter but more built, with a trucker hat over his short black hair, comes over, holding out a bottle of beer to each of us. Jamie introduces him as Gus, Rosie's boyfriend. The beer is ice cold, but Jamie and Gus are immediately friendly.

"So how do you know Lani?" Gus asks.

"We're secretly married."

There's a moment of silence and then the laughter starts.

"Wow, way to go for it," Gus says. He smiles with even white teeth and raises his bottle of beer to me in a toast.

"I knew Lani had some big secret. Must have been you," Jamie says.

"Seriously, though, how did you meet?" Gus asks.

"We met in college. I was a lowly freshman who didn't know

any better than to ask out the cute junior girl in his intro to film class."

"You and Lani dated in college?" Jamie asks. "What was your major?"

"English," I confess.

"Same as Ophelia." He glances over at his girl, and his eyes go dopey for a second behind his angular glasses.

"I think she was a couple of years behind me."

"She says her students love your books. I think we carry a couple of titles in the museum gift shop."

"Which museum?"

"The Fox Museum of Science and Innovation. If you haven't been back to Santa Barbara since you graduated, you wouldn't know about it. It opened a few years ago. I'm the head of the maker space. You should come by and check it out."

My list of Santa Barbara sights to see is growing longer.

"I will. Lani said you work at a botanical garden?" I say to Gus.

"Pacifica Park. If you have time to come by some afternoon, I can give you a tour."

"I don't know if I'll have time on this trip, but I'm—" I hesitate, but why the hell shouldn't I tell them? "I'm going to be moving back to California pretty soon. So I'll make it a priority."

"What brings you back?"

"Oh, you know, the usual. Disillusionment. Existential crisis. I moved to New York to be the next great American novelist and I write 32-page picture books instead. It's time for a change of scene."

"And a change of company?" Gus nods at Lani, who has acquired a glass of iced tea and is laughing along with Rosie at something Ophelia is saying.

Lani is the most beautiful woman at a party populated with plenty of good-looking women. She's the brightest light on the patio and I'm a hapless moth. I'm the schmuck who was lucky enough to come with her to this party, but who let her go so long ago that even if we haven't severed our connection legally, time's grown such thick scar tissue over the wound that maybe there's no way to start fresh.

And yet. There's something between us time hasn't been able to erase. Seeing her with her friends and her friends' partners—there has to be a reason she's only had short-term relationships since us. She never replaced me. Did I burn her that badly? Or is there a chance I could try to get this right the second time around?

I realize belatedly the conversation has gone on without me. I tune back in to hear Gus say, "Oh yeah, I see it now." He elbows Jamie in the side. "You were right."

"Told you. Takes one to know one." Jamie shrugs. "Poor sap."

"Who's a poor sap?" I ask, though I suspect I know the answer.

"Jamie here thinks you're into our girl Lani. I was holding back my opinion but then I saw the way you can't stop looking at her and I have to admit he has a point. You're done for, bro."

I half-heartedly object. "Me? And Lani?" As embarrassing as it is to be immediately called out by two guys I just met and who in a perfect world would become my friends, they aren't wrong.

"It's okay, we've been there. But I have to warn you, Lani's really not into long-term relationships," Jamie says.

"But neither was Rosie. Or Ophelia. Or Kate. So, you know, there's hope," Gus says, clapping me on the shoulder. "If that's what you're after."

"I'm not after anything. Lani and I have a...complicated history. Though, if nothing else, we're trying to be friends again."

"Friends?" Jamie's eyebrows hit the fringe of his floppy hair.

"The way you look at her is not very friendly. And I should know. I was in the friend zone for two very long years, Reed."

"Two years?" I glance at Ophelia, then back at Jamie. "Wow. That's a long time."

"It was pure torture. But I'd have waited twice as long. Three times," Jamie says.

I get where he's coming from. "She's worth it, right?"

"A hundred percent," he says.

Across the yard, Lani's got her head huddled with her friends. Her face is so familiar to me, but every time I see her I get a jolt of longing so fierce it's almost like being zapped by the third rail. I'd be a fool not to ask her for another chance. Haven't we both waited long enough?

I turn to Jamie and Gus. They're looking at me with identical expressions, a mixture of pity and understanding. Gus claps me on the shoulder again and intones gravely, "Good luck, dude."

I'm clearly going to need it.

CHAPTER 13
LANI

I sip my iced tea and try not to worry that Reed might inadvertently tell everyone we're married. Rosie's telling us an amusing story from her week at work at the hospital in Ventura, but I'm only half-listening.

"It's weird not being pinged three times a day by Nicole this weekend," Rosie says. "You think she and Ricky are doing okay with their digital detox?"

"I wonder if they were tired of having sex by the first night or the second," I say.

"What are you talking about?" Ophelia says. "Why would they get tired of that?"

"I don't know. They've been together for like, a decade. Don't you think they know everything about each other by this point?"

"What's gotten into you tonight? You know, some people don't get bored with one sexual partner after three rounds," O says.

I'm in a prickly mood and even though she isn't wrong, her tone stings. "I'm sorry. I'm a little stressed out. With Reed here and him meeting everyone."

"I haven't met him yet," Rosie complains. "But it looks like he's getting along like a house on fire with the boys."

I glance over at Reed, who is deep in conversation with Gus and Jamie. They look natural, a group of three attractive men sipping beer and shooting the shit. It's strange to have a guy of my own—usually I go to these group events solo. Reed's not mine, exactly, but still, it's kind of nice.

"Food's ready," Jamie's mom calls, and we all drift over to load our plates with too much of everything.

Reed finds me in the line and we sit next to each other at one of the picnic tables set up on the flagstone patio. Rosie and Gus settle down across from us, so I introduce an impatient Rosie to Reed.

"I haven't read any of your books, but my niece's birthday is coming up, so now I know what to get her," Rosie says. "Is it true you modeled the main character on Lani?"

I bite my tongue by mistake and curse.

"Are you okay?" Reed asks, looking at me with concern.

I wave him away. "Fine. Fine." When did O have a chance to tell Rosie about that?

"Well, Lucy was unquestionably inspired by Lani in some ways," Reed admits. "But they have some differences."

"Like what?" Rosie asks innocently.

"Lucy's a lot shorter," Reed deadpans.

I scoff.

"Gus's nephew is a big reader. I'll have to make sure his moms show him your books, if they haven't already."

"That's so nice of you." Reed looks a tad overwhelmed by the attention. I'm just glad they aren't grilling him about our relationship.

The conversation moves on to neutral topics like Ophelia and Jamie's progress with their special project to install maker labs at every elementary school in the district, and Pacifica Park's new program, led by Gus, to bring in teens who need to fulfill community service hours by having them work in the garden, and at the same time giving them basic plant knowledge and gardening skills.

I feel guilty that my friends are making such a big effort to include him while I haven't been honest with them. And I wonder why Reed fitting in so well with the group makes me equal parts happy and uncomfortable. This is a one-off, right? No need to get worked up over it either way.

The group breaks up after a while when our hosts bring out the dessert. Reed hovers until Laura gives him the thumbs-up on the pie, then he seems to relax, falling into conversation with Rory, who I recall is a really big fan of young adult books.

On impulse, I snap a candid picture of the group with my phone and send it to Nicole and Kate with a brief "Miss you."

"You know, I don't think Reed's over you."

"What are you talking about?" I look up from my phone to Ophelia's face, adorned with a teasing smile.

"The way he looks at you," Ophelia says. "Serious heart eyes."

"Come on." We might have come to this party together, but we're not a couple. We're barely friends. I don't want to know how he looks at me. It's too dangerous.

"Well, I'm glad you brought him, anyway. Jamie and Gus are in love, I'm pretty sure."

"Well, they're going to get their hearts broken. He's going back to New York in a few days."

"I'll tell Jamie not to get his hopes up that Reed might move back."

My sentiments exactly. "Shouldn't you be heading home? It's a school night," I remind her lightly.

She backs off, thankfully, and nods. "Sure. See you soon, Lani."

I give her a hug and collect my salad bowl, which, as I predicted, is nearly empty. Laura resists my attempts to get her to keep the leftovers. I'm about to head to the car to be rid of it, when Reed materializes at my elbow.

"Ready to split?" he asks.

"Ready if you are." We say our goodbyes on the way out.

"Let's go by your house on the way home."

"Really? You want to see it again?" I haven't driven by all weekend, nor have I heard from Beverly. I need to see it to remind myself that it's a real place that exists outside of my imagination.

"Let's do it."

"Okay." It's not far, maybe ten minutes. I suppose I could make conversation, but I'm tired and Reed seems to have something on his mind.

I put the car in neutral at the curb in front of the property, taking my foot off the clutch and engaging the e-break. The house looks the same as it did two nights ago—dark and in need of attention. I want it to be mine so bad I can taste it.

"Why did you pick this house, Lani?"

"Didn't you ask me that before?"

"I wondered if you saw the resemblance. Remember the house we used to drive past on the way to hike in the foothills? That place was farther north, but it was a Craftsman, like this one."

Suddenly, I know what he's talking about. It was a cute little house, tidy, and in much better shape than this one, with a similar wraparound porch. Every time we'd drive by, we'd wave, and Reed would say things like, "I'm going to write a bestseller and buy you a house like this one." I'd counter with, "I'm going to be the CEO of some cool start-up and buy *you* a house like this." Because we could never let things be without pushing against each other, without negotiating the terms and conditions of everything, including our dreams.

But no, I'd honestly forgotten about that until now. Only

maybe I hadn't. Maybe on some level I chose this house because of those associations.

"Goddamn it," I snarl, suddenly disgusted with my lack of self-awareness.

"What?"

"I thought I was buying my dream house," I say irritably. "But it turns out I'm buying *our* dream house."

CHAPTER 14

LANI

I pull away from my—our?—house slowly, strangely reluctant to end the evening. It scares me how easily I've slipped back into being part of a we. I've been determinedly single for six uninterrupted years. I'd pretty much resigned myself to being a sassy single lady, dating when I want, sleeping with whomever I want, and never, ever being a part of a we again.

I hadn't been sad about it. I like being by myself. I like living alone. I like the freedom to come and go without anyone else getting a say.

My mom likes to say that Kalama women love men, but we love ourselves more. She says it like it's a given, that we're supposed to put ourselves first, that we're better off on our own. I guess I started believing her after Dad left, but it wasn't until Reed left for Iowa that my buy-in was complete.

Then why is it so easy to be with Reed? Is it because being with him takes me back to a different, simpler time? Because he reminds me of being young and stupidly in love? Despite the years, neither of us has changed so much, and we're falling back into the same patterns that made us a good fit from the start.

I never thought of us as particularly compatible back then. But now I see our similarities, not our differences. He's a decent, kind person who has also spent a lot of time on his own. We both like food and movies and books and drawing and design.

And sex.

At a stoplight, I notice him spinning the leather strap around his wrist. I reach out, touching it lightly, feeling the heat of his skin underneath.

"Is this the same one?" He wore a similar bracelet in college, a gift from his sister when he left for school.

"No. That one finally wore out. I found this in a shop in the city."

"Suits you." Sometimes manly jewelry speaks of trying too hard.

"I like your jewelry, too," he says. "No rings, though."

The light changes to green and I let my foot off the clutch. I glance down at my hands resting on the steering wheel. They're typically bare; I embellish with nail polish.

"No, I don't wear rings."

"But you still have it?"

I know what he means. The ring we picked out in the lobby of the Reno chapel, a plain gold-plated band.

"I think so," I say lightly, though I know full well where it is, nestled in a leather pouch in the top drawer of my dresser. "What about you?"

We'd gotten him a similar, thicker ring. I liked the way it looked on his wide, strong fingers.

"Someplace," he says absently. I'm positive he knows exactly where it is, just as I do. We're awful liars.

"You want to come back to my place?" Shit. I've used the line so many times, it simply slips out.

"Why?"

I've never gotten that response before. Usually the guy I'm

with is falling all over himself to accompany me home for whatever I let him do.

"Why?" I repeat, my voice full of disbelief.

He laughs. "You want to play Monopoly?"

Now it's my turn to laugh. I flash back to one of our first dates. We'd spent the evening at a predictably mediocre student play one of our friends had a small part in. We suffered through the pretentious storyline and the wooden blocking and then stood around on the sidewalk outside, pretending we hadn't hated it in case the other one had thought it was subversively brilliant or some other hot take.

I'd gotten fed up with the charade and finally said, "That was shit."

Reed grinned and said, "You want to come over and play Monopoly?"

"Sure, if you want to lose," I said. We got as far as building a few houses before we started making out all over the board. That was the first time we slept together. In the years after, we'd use it as a code for having sex. One of those little in-jokes you develop when you're really close with someone.

His using it now makes me sad I haven't had anyone to share inside jokes with since he left. Makes me wish so many years hadn't passed without us being able to joke with each other again.

Makes me want to play Monopoly with him again. Right now.

"I guess I'm up for some Monopoly," I say slowly. I forget about taking him back to his place and head for my apartment.

"Wait, really?" He sounds surprised.

Fuck. Was he joking? "Um." I'm on the verge of blushing with embarrassment, but then I remember I don't get shamed about sex. Not by Reed. Not by anyone. I straighten my shoulders. "Yes, really. If you're interested." I haven't met very many people who aren't. Then again, with Reed it's not my normal straightforward hookup.

Still, sex is sex.

"Just one night?" he asks.

"Consider it marital privileges," I say. "No expectations."

"For fun?"

"Yeah. Fun. Like Monopoly."

He's quiet for a minute, as if judging how serious I am. Since I'm perennially not serious about sex, I shouldn't be holding my breath waiting for his answer. This is just another one-night stand. I've had plenty. I know how they work, and I know how to make them effective. The fact that we had sex about a million times a million years ago doesn't really factor in.

"I'll do it on one condition."

"Which is?"

"I get to spend the night. No kicking me out at three in the morning."

The morning after doesn't have to be awkward, but I do usually try to engineer an early departure for my guests. Rarely do they turn into overnight stays. How does he know that?

I shrug. "Fine. You can sleep over."

"Are you still on the pill?" he asks.

"Jesus, Reed."

"What? I'm doing my due diligence."

"I'm on birth control, yes. And I always use condoms, even for oral. What about you?"

"Doesn't the latex taste gross?"

"I found some nonlubricated ones that work for me," I say. "And answer the question."

"Yes, I always used a condom. And it's been a while, as we already established. I had all my blood work done at my last physical. So I'm perfectly healthy."

"That's good to hear."

With that business out of the way, we spend the rest of the drive in silence. It's a good thing I drive these streets every day because I'm on complete autopilot wondering what's going to happen when we get back to my place.

Is it going to be like riding a bike? Will his body feel the same? Will he make me feel the same as he used to? Or is it going to be like being with someone entirely new?

I realize I'm nervous. And I'm never nervous about sex.

I've got it down to a science: When you're with someone new, it's all about managing expectations. I have a few dependable go-to moves, and when guys see I'm up for items on the menu beyond the tried-and-true, it either lowers their inhibitions and we can really have some fun, or it makes them feel inadequate and they seize up. Which is why alcohol is usually part of the mix. They don't call it a social lubricant for nothing.

But Reed and I haven't been drinking. Maybe we should open a bottle of wine when we get there. I park, racking my brain to think if I have any decent bottles in the house.

"Lani? Hello?" Reed's hand is on my arm. I realize I've been staring into space.

"Oh sorry." I make a move to get out, but he stops me.

"You okay? We can actually play Monopoly if you want."

Suddenly, I feel like a teenager again, clumsy and virginal. Why does Reed have the power to make me feel this way after all this time? This was my idea, but why? Because I thought it would help when he left again to have the fresh memory of his body against mine for another six years' worth of fantasies? I'm really shit for brains tonight.

"Look, I know it seems like I have everything together—and I do!" I insist rather pathetically. Reed just smiles indulgently, which both melts my heart and adds steel to my spine, confusingly. "But sometimes I take spontaneity too far." It's as far as I'm willing to go to admit I hadn't thought my offer all the way through.

"It's okay. Let's go inside. We can talk."

"Talk?" It feels like all we've done is talk since he got here.

"Yeah, talk. Or, I don't know. Have a drink?"

"Yes. A drink." I latch onto the activity. Drinking leads to kissing which leads to sex. But we're both adults. If we don't like it, we can stop. Isn't that what people who don't have problems say? I can stop at any time.

With Reed, it seems I don't know that I can.

CHAPTER 15

REED

Lani's place is just as homey as before. Now that I've seen her dream house—our dream house?—I'm noticing she maybe has a bit too much crammed in this apartment. She could use more space. She could have a little room for a studio. She needs a bigger kitchen so she can spread out when she cooks.

I'm in awe of the life she's built for herself, and I'm sad I've missed all this time with her. I don't know the story behind the glass chicken on her bookshelf or where she got the pretty little watercolor hanging on the wall to the right of the kitchen sink.

Why did I think it was such a hot idea to spend the better part of a decade apart from her? That's time we'll never get back. I know there's something to be said for it making us the people we've become, but I liked Lani before, too.

That ambitious, smart, funny girl is still there, if a bit shellacked to a hard shine by time and having to do absolutely everything for herself, every minute of the day.

"Want some wine?" Lani has been bouncing back and forth all night. She'd basically been lost in space back in the car, now she's buzzing around, grabbing a corkscrew, glasses. She rummages around in a little refrigerator I only now notice tucked in a corner of her kitchen.

"What's that?"

"A wine fridge."

"Why do you have a wine fridge?"

"It was Nicole's Christmas present last year. Not sure why she thought I needed one, but I'm chalking it up to her wanting her chardonnay chilled to the perfect temperature whenever she comes over, rather than her making a statement about how much wine I drink. Red okay?"

"Sure." I don't really need a drink, but it's clear she's not as comfortable with the idea of us playing Monopoly as she seemed at first. Honestly, she's the most beautiful person in the world, and it's been a really long time since I've slept with anyone, but the last thing I want to do is fuck up our already insane relationship even more. And sex is like the number one way to fuck up relationships.

I take the glass she offers me and sip the peppery wine. "This is really good. When did you start drinking wine, anyway?"

"Nicole and Ricky are the kind of people who host un-ironic wine tastings. One year for her birthday, Nicole took a bunch of us to Paso Robles to tour wineries. It was actually pretty fun."

If I hadn't just met some of her friends and seen for myself how down-to-earth they are, I'd be doubting my ability to keep up with her new Santa Barbara circle. Nicole sounds like the kind of person we used to make fun of in college—the spoiled rich bitch whose parents were paying for college and their apartment in Isla Vista, probably paying their credit card bills, too, maxed out on trips to Costco for handles of vodka and cases of kombucha.

She takes a gulp of her wine and sits in her blue armchair, unstrapping her high heels. I'm too keyed up to sit. I find myself by her bookshelf and pull down the first Reed and Lucy book. It's in good shape, but when I open it, the spine doesn't crack. She's obviously read it.

If I'm going to get Lani to give me a real chance, even if all I end up getting is a goodbye kiss, she needs to know the whole story.

"Do you know how hard it is to get a contract for a children's book in traditional publishing these days?"

She shakes her head.

"Really hard. It's tough to break out, and almost impossible without an agent."

"So how did you do it?"

"I got an agent." I sigh. "I told you basically what happened in Iowa, but I haven't told you much about New York."

"I'm listening." She tucks her bare feet underneath her as if waiting for me to tell her a story.

"My MFA advisor was very old-school. She thought all great writers need to suffer, and there's no better place to suffer than New York City. My thesis novel wasn't generating any interest from agents, and I didn't feel like I could come back here." I glance at Lani, but her face is neutral.

"I had enough cash for a one-way plane ticket and a month's security deposit on a room in a Queens sublet. I had no job prospects. I barely had any marketable skills. Even if MFAs weren't a dime a dozen, it's not like I knew how to make spreadsheets. I thought about applying for a job in publishing, but I didn't want to get stuck reading other people's work instead of writing my own. But it turned out I couldn't get a job doing anything."

It had been more than a little dispiriting. I'd been afraid I might have to call my parents and ask for money, which would have been humiliating. "One of my roommates had been a temp, and he got me a spot with his old agency. To be a temp worker you actually have to have qualifications, but he helped me massage the application. Eventually I was at least able to make enough to pay my meager bills. So there I was, my first winter in New York, freezing, writing a self-indulgently shitty novel in my free time, which I had a fair amount of because I didn't have any friends. I was suffering all right. My MFA advisor would have been so proud."

"Wow, I had no idea," Lani says. "That sounds really difficult."

"To get out of my apartment, I'd go to the library. One of the children's librarians saw my drawings, got me thinking about writing a story to go with them. Around the same time, I did a temp job for a publisher, which is how I met Erin. She saw the story, sent it to her friend Kingston, and he helped me turn it into a pitch. At first I was skeptical, because I was a 'real' writer, right, not a picture book author."

"You know you are a real author, though," Lani says. "It doesn't matter if the books have five hundred words or fifty thousand."

"So everyone keeps telling me. But knowing something and feeling it are sometimes two different things."

She looks like she wants to say more, but she nods. "So how did you sell the book?"

"Kingston sold *Reed and Lucy Go to the Beach* in a three-book deal at auction. Auction! There was more than one house that wanted the series." I remember when Kingston told me what the highest offer was, how when I did the math it was more money than I'd made cumulatively in my life to date. "Once I had deadlines and contracts and promotion to do, things started getting better. I kept temping for a while, even though I was so bad at it, and I still live in that terrible apartment. I guess even once the money started coming in, I wasn't sure it would last."

Children's book authors usually can't make enough to live on through their books alone, but I've been lucky. Reed and

Lucy have a big enough following that Kingston, clever man that he is, has gotten me foreign rights contracts, a television show option, and merchandising deals. It all adds up, even after his cut. If I keep churning out Reed and Lucy books, and, more importantly, if the public keeps buying them, I'll never be a starving artist again.

What's ironic about the whole thing is that my publishing success was practically a fluke and had nothing whatsoever to do with my time in the MFA program.

"What happened when the book came out?" Lani asks.

"At first I was so busy doing promo and working on the second book that I forgot people were actually going to read it. And then I started getting letters from kids and parents and librarians, and wow, hearing that they liked Reed and Lucy was fucking unreal. So, even if I'm not the writer I thought I would be, I'd be an entitled, arrogant jerk not to appreciate my success. I'd like to think I'm not entirely a lost cause."

"You've never been a lost cause, Reed," she murmurs. "It sounds like even though things haven't turned out how you thought they would, you ended up finding a purpose."

I look over at Lani sitting there, effortlessly magnificent, and my gut aches for what I've lost. "A purpose but not a place. I've been wandering ever since I left here. I want to come home."

She was my home, once upon a time. I thought she'd be it for my happily ever after, too. But that, like so many things, didn't turn out how I thought it would, and I'm still looking for a place to genuinely belong.

"Hey, it's late," she says, rising out of her chair like a cat. She holds out a hand to me. "We didn't get to Monopoly, but let's go to bed."

CHAPTER 16

LANI

It's not like I never let guys sleep over. I just tacitly encourage them to fuck me, then get out.

Last night, I handed Reed a freebie toothbrush imprinted with my dentist's name and turned down the side of the bed he used to take. I'd lost my nerve when it came to having sex with him, but I couldn't kick him out after that sad story. I had no idea the years had been so difficult for him. I had sort of imagined him swinging onto the publishing scene and getting offers left and right, not working for fifteen dollars an hour as a temp and falling ass-backwards into writing a children's book. While living in Queens. With roommates.

We lay side by side, and it wasn't as uncomfortable as I thought it would be to turn over and whisper goodnight before falling asleep.

Waking up facing Reed, I can make out the dark brown stubble on his jaw and upper lip. His chest hair peeks out of the V-neck of the white undershirt he wore to bed. There's no doubt he's different than The Boy. He's older. He seems a little wiser. He's hotter, which is annoying. His chest is a taut wall beneath the soft cotton of his T-shirt, his arms stretching the sleeves.

It's strange to have him in my life at all, a real person with real problems, rather than the version of Reed I've had in my head all this time. That Reed was the one I was heartbroken over, then hated, then bestowed a neutral good place in my head. I'm beginning to understand the peace I made with Reed was one-sided. We haven't been real to each other for so long. We've both been living with a memory, and a fantasy. I need to make peace with the real Reed, or he's going to hurt me all over again.

I don't want to hurt him, either.

The idea of sleeping with him—well, we just slept together, so that's done. But sex—it's a monumentally bad proposition. I had been taken with the idea that we could pretend our baggage had sailed off with the tide and we could indulge ourselves. But Reed's different, for so many reasons, from the guys I take home. He'll never be one and done for me. And I don't want him to be.

The problem is we have these few days and then he's gone. Can we come to a better understanding before he leaves and I never see him again?

He's sleeping soundly. I ease out of bed and throw on what I think of as my robe, a faded gray cardigan that hits me mid-thigh. I pull my hair back with a scrunchie, mentally planning my outfit for the day. I usually figure out what I'm going to wear the night before but having an overnight guest has thrown off my routine.

Once in the kitchen, I start the coffee—priorities—then set water to boil for poached eggs. I have all the salad leftovers from last night in the fridge, so I refresh the greens for a breakfast salad. By the time I'm sliding the eggs expertly into the water, the air smells like coffee and Reed has appeared in his T-shirt, jeans pulled on over his boxers, barefoot. His hair is mussed and he looks soft. He's not a teddy bear, but he kind of looks like one. I resist the urge to cross the room and nestle myself in his arms.

"Morning. Coffee?"

"Please." His voice is sleep-rough, which activates a different part of my attraction to him. How can he transform from teddy bear to sex object with one word? "Is that breakfast?"

I pass him a mug and check the timer. "Eggs will be done in a minute."

"You're so good at this."

"You're going to have to be more specific. There are a lot of things I'm good at."

"Adulting. You're a pro. You're a living *Sunset* magazine article, with your houseplants and your poached eggs and your awesome creative job."

"And you're an Instagram wet dream with your picture books and your man jewelry and your gritty New York existence."

I push his, yes, expertly plated California-style breakfast toward him and dig into my own.

Reed takes a bite and moans. "This is really good."

"Thank you. I have to go to work pretty soon, but you're welcome to hang here if you want."

"No, that's okay. I need to work today, too. I need my computer and my sketchbook."

"Sounds good." We eat in silence for a while. It's nice having someone else to cook for. Most mornings I quickly grab a green juice and a hard-boiled egg, but this is surprisingly pleasant, if a little cramped, both of us sitting side by side at the breakfast bar in the patch of sun streaming through my kitchen window. I think about the kitchen at the house, how it's twice the size of this one, with the attached dining room I plan to completely renovate. There's a spare room off the dining room that I was going to use for a pantry, but it would actually make a cozy office for someone. If we expanded the back porch, we could even bump the room out a little and turn it into more of a studio. There's nice light on that side of the house.

I blink, utterly carried away by my fantasy. I don't need a studio. And I was *not* imagining a space where Reed could write and work. I swear.

"Would it be okay if I stopped by your shop later today?" Reed asks. "If you're busy, you don't have to worry about me. But I'd like to see it."

"Oh sure. It's open until six on Mondays."

"Awesome."

"I better get dressed." I'm strangely reluctant to leave this domestic bubble, even though I have a hundred things to do today. Usually I'm anxious to get to the office and be around other humans. With Reed here, my need for interaction is already sated.

"I'll clean up," Reed offers. "After I finish my coffee."

"Deal." My phone buzzes before I can get off my stool. It's my Realtor. "Gotta take this. Hey, Beverly."

"Beverly?" Reed mouths questioningly.

I listen for a minute. "Oh. They counteroffered?"

Reed's forehead wrinkles as he blatantly eavesdrops on my side of the conversation. I turn my back to him so I can concentrate. "And when do they need to know by?" Beverly explains the timeline and I thank her and tell her I'll let her know soon.

I put the phone down.

"What is it? Bad news?" Reed asks, concerned.

"The sellers didn't accept my offer. They counteroffered, but it's more than I wanted to pay. I have to let them know by the end of the day." I'm disappointed, even though I knew this was a possible outcome.

"But if you accept their counteroffer, they have to sell it to you, and the house is yours," Reed says.

"True. But if I meet their price, I'll basically be using all of my savings on the down payment. I won't have any cash left for any of the improvements I wanted to make. I'd have to get a construction loan or something and taking on more debt is really not something I wanted to do."

"I see. How much is the difference?" Reed's voice is suddenly businesslike.

"They want twenty-five thousand more than I offered. It's a lot." Still less than the asking price, which was totally over-reaching considering the state of the place. I might splurge once in a while on a fantastic piece of art or timeless jewelry, but at heart I'm a thrifty girl with an eye for a bargain. Spending a dime more than I have to on anything offends me, especially when it feels like such a leap to have so much money tied up in something like a house. The most expensive thing I've ever owned is my car, and this is an entirely different league.

I've been staring into space clutching my phone for a while when Reed's hand is suddenly on my arm, warm and comforting. "Hey, is there anything I can do to help?"

"What? No. I have to go over the numbers again, decide if I should counteroffer, take the deal, or let it go." I swallow against the lump in my throat. Dammit. I'd let myself get too attached to the place, even knowing it might not work out. Very unlike me.

"You want to talk it out?" He's still here. It feels weird. I'm used to doing things on my own, especially when it comes to money. He and I never shared a bank account or expenses. We always paid our own way for everything, even when it didn't always make sense.

"Um, no thank you. I've got to get to work. Stay as long as you want. Maybe I'll see you later at the shop."

"Are you sure?"

"I'm going to be late." I practically run to my bedroom, taking my clothes off as I move. I've got a thousand thoughts in my head, and even though I'm the boss and there's no one to give me a hard time except myself, I hate being late. I dress in record time, simple black slacks and a purple sleeveless blouse. I put on my chunkiest gold jewelry. Maybe if I look like a queen, I'll attract queen energy.

I swipe on some mascara, purple eyeshadow, and lip gloss, grab my purse, my phone charger, and an apple. Reed is in the kitchen, cleaning up our dishes. He's put some alt rock on my smart speaker and he looks like a picture of domesticity. My stomach flips with some kind of premonition. I see us, in the future, sharing breakfast before I head to the office, leaving Reed to tidy up before he heads to his studio to write. I come home and relax by making us dinner, Reed telling me about his day before we spend the night watching the latest binge-worthy show, slowly making love before we fall asleep in each other's arms. Scary how easily I can see it. Scary how right it feels.

Scary, period.

"I'll see you later?" I'm suddenly shy. Just because I can see Reed slotting into my life here doesn't mean he feels the same way. He may not love New York, but it's his home, the cradle of his career.

"Listen, Lani, let me know if you'd rather talk about this later, but I was thinking maybe I could help with the house."

"How?"

"I could give you the difference for your down payment. Then you can do your repairs without taking on more debt. I'd simply get the money wired."

"Excuse me?" I'm having trouble processing.

"Twenty-five thousand, right? I know how much you love that house. The moment I saw it, I knew it was supposed to be yours. I would really love it if you'd let me do this."

"You want me to let you give me twenty-five thousand dollars? Didn't you spend last night telling me you were the poster boy for struggling artists?"

"I was until a couple of years ago. Kingston's the best—he's sold TV rights, foreign rights, merchandising, the whole nine. I could have moved to my own place a while ago, but I didn't have much of a reason to. I hate New York. But you, Lani, you have this amazing life here. I'm so proud of you. You should have this. I want you to. And God knows I never gave you anywhere near what you deserved when we were together. You deserve this."

"I don't think you giving me money is really appropriate." Our relationship was never about transactions. It doesn't seem right to bring something like this into the complex web we're already navigating.

"You could think of it as a fee for letting me profit off our history. A share of the royalties from Reed and Lucy. I couldn't have written those without you, after all."

I narrow my eyes at him. "I highly doubt your agent or your lawyer would want you saying stuff like that."

"Why? You going to sue me?" He smiles at me, lopsided. "Let's settle out of court. How does twenty-five thousand sound?"

"Stop it. Be serious." I'm uncomfortable with the idea of taking his money, but the pragmatic side of me does see the appeal in having this problem solved so neatly. I could accept the counteroffer and be one step closer to the house of my dreams. I could always pay him back.

"I am serious. Look, take some time to think about it." He leans against the counter, the sunshine coming in the kitchen window backlighting him and giving him a golden aura. "You'd be doing me a favor."

"Stop bullshitting me," I say, but my tone is mild. If Reed is one thing, it's a good guy. He'd probably make the same offer to any of his friends if he could help. And we're friends. Sort of.

"I'll come by the shop later and we can call my bank together."

"I doubt it would have to happen that quickly," I admit. "I have the cash to increase the binder."

"Even better. You want to call Beverly now and tell her to accept the counteroffer?"

"No. I have to get to work, for real. But I'll think about it. And I'll let you know."

"Okay."

It's a good thing the kitchen bar blocks my way to him, or I'd have a really hard time not giving him a hug goodbye. But I do let myself smile at him. "Thanks, Reed."

My thoughts are full of pros and cons the entire drive to work.

CHAPTER 17
REED

Winesap Design is in a stand-alone building on a shady side street not far from Wild Child Café, where I spent my morning making a little progress on my draft of *Reed and Lucy Go to School*. It's styled like a beach house, painted a warm gray with white trim. The building is bifurcated—the front looks like the retail shop, and the back must be where Lani and Nicole have their offices. But where do they do their manufacturing? There's a ton I don't understand about their business.

I'd worry about them having to depend on foot traffic this far off the main tourist drag, but as I approach on foot myself, I can tell random passersby aren't really their clientele. The parking lot is full of shiny, expensive vehicles, and there's a van with the logo of an interior design firm emblazoned on the side.

I walk up the sedge-lined flagstone walkway and enter through the main door. It's a fairly small space, but the high ceilings make it feel airy, even though every surface is covered in rich, textured pieces, from pillows like the ones decorating Lani's sofa, to dishes, candles, and jewelry. One corner is hung floor to ceiling with wallpaper samples, and another has what looks like an old-fashioned writing desk with cubbyholes filled with different types of stationery. There's also furniture—chairs and tables, even a hammock.

I might have thought the place would be empty at two o'clock on a Monday afternoon, but it's buzzing with activity. A skinny guy in glasses scribbles furiously on a tablet while a middle-aged woman in an honest-to-God kaftan points at items.

"That one, and that one. Two of these. And you're sure you can have all of it there by tomorrow morning?"

"No problem, Magda," the man says. "We'll load up the truck this afternoon."

"That's why I love you, darling," she says, giving him an exaggerated air kiss.

I turn away from that spectacle to see a young woman sit down at the stationery, um, station?, with another young person who clearly works here.

"Let me show you the engagement announcement designs we have on file. Of course, you can commission something completely original if you don't see anything you like."

"This is so exciting," the woman says. "I'm completely in love with the aloe prints. I love them almost as much as I love my fiancé."

I smile. Wow. This isn't like any random shop. The people who come here are actual fans. Interesting.

"Can I help you?" Yet another employee—how many people work here?—comes up to me as I'm looking at a display of jewelry. A pretty pendant catches my eye. The warm brown stone in the gold setting makes me think of Lani.

"Hi, first time here. Just taking it all in."

"Welcome to Winesap Design," she says smoothly. She's slim and her long blond hair is loose. She's wearing some kind of trendy jumpsuit and has enormous diamond studs in her ears. How much do they pay their sales associates? "Were you looking for something special?"

"I was hoping to see Lani Kalama, if she's available."

"Lani?" Her expression turns curious. "She's not here at the moment, but I can leave her a message."

"Oh." I'm disappointed to miss her. My fingers reach out to touch the pendant of their own accord.

"See something you like?"

"This is nice."

The woman hums. "Those are from a new designer, Janice Sunshine. I love that line."

"I thought everything in here was designed by Nicole Winesap."

She laughs. "Goodness, no, I wouldn't have the time. Of course, I do a lot of the design work, but a good amount of what we carry here is curated from different local designers."

"You're Nicole?" I take her in with fresh eyes. Now that I know who she is, I can match the description to the impression I've gotten of her and I'm a bit surprised. I'd imagined someone more bohemian, maybe zanier, but she's as professional and impeccably turned out as Lani always is.

"Nicole Winesap, nice to meet you." She offers me a hand, which I take.

"I'm Reed Bennet."

Her eyes widen slightly when I say my name. "Not the Reed Bennet about whom I had a stack of notifications waiting for me when I finally turned my cell back on this morning? My cousin Ophelia sent me a dozen texts. You're a writer?"

"I write and illustrate children's books," I clarify. Not that writer doesn't also fit, but whatever.

"She said you're coming to her school tomorrow. That's really generous, Reed."

"I'm here as part of a book tour; it wasn't hard to squeeze in another stop. My publisher usually sets me up at bookstores, but schools are way more fun."

"I have to confess I haven't read any of your books, but I

don't have any kids. No nieces and nephews, either. But my friend Kate is pregnant, so I'll have to get your books for her as a baby gift."

Kate is the one who's out of town, I seem to remember. "So maybe you could tell Lani I stopped by?"

"Of course. You're welcome to wait. She's on a run to the bank. She'll probably be back in a flash."

"Oh okay, sure." I haven't heard from Lani all day, but I did call my own bank to learn the easiest way to transfer money from my account to Lani's. I've thought about it all day, but I'm no less certain I want to give her the money for her house than I was when the idea first struck me this morning.

"Want to come back to the workshop?"

"Absolutely."

We pass behind the jewelry counter, go through a door, and I find myself in a small office with lockers and a microwave.

"The employee area," Nicole says as she leads me into another, larger room. "This is the storeroom." It's bigger than I would have imagined looking at the building from the front, with floor-to-ceiling shelves full of overstock. The storeroom opens up into another sizable space furnished with a couple of desks, a drafting table, a sewing table, and a wall of fabric samples and other materials.

"Wow, it's like your own personal arts and crafts store in here."

She grins. "Why do you think I got into this business? I can write off all the glue guns and pipe cleaners I want."

"Cool. So, if this is your workshop area, where you do the manufacturing?"

"I own another building a couple of blocks away where we have six full-time craftspeople. We fabricate some of the pieces there, some we outsource, and some we only license the designs for and don't have a hand in the production at all."

"Complicated."

"Lani thrives on complicated. She runs this place like a machine."

"I'll bet."

"Seriously, she's expanding our footprint almost faster than I can keep up. That's why we started carrying more designers in the shop. We do a decent business, but the retail side is more for testing ideas and having a presence in the community."

I walk over to the drafting table. It's covered in a series of drawings of multicolored beach pebbles.

"I'm working on a new wallpaper pattern. Part of our beach themes for next summer."

"Next summer?"

"We work about nine months ahead of the season here."

"Have you seen Lani's shell sketches? They would be a good fit for a beach theme."

Nicole squints at me. "Lani's sketches?"

I'm aware Lani would have shown Nicole her sketches if she'd wanted to, but I figure there's no harm in letting Nicole know Lani has an eye for more than numbers and operations. "She's a talented artist. We used to go down to the Rincon and sketch for hours."

"How long have you known Lani?"

"About ten years."

"Huh. Strange she's never mentioned you." She's got a gleam in her eyes that sets off my internal alarm. Clearly her instincts that something else is going on have been aroused.

"I've been living in New York," I say hastily. "Only in town for a few days."

"I used to live in New York," she says, taking the bait. "Chelsea. What about you?"

"Queens," I respond flatly.

"Oh." She recovers quickly. "Well, I'm so glad you were able to squeeze in a visit on your book tour. You and Lani should come to dinner with me and my husband tonight. Do you like seafood?"

"Reed?" Lani saves me from answering by stepping through a back door, svelte and glamorous, pushing oversized sunglasses onto the top of her head.

"Hey. I decided to stop by and see the operation. It's impressive what you've got going on here."

"Reed was telling me about some sketches of yours he thought would be a good fit for the beach line. Did you want to show me those?"

Lani was clearly not expecting that. Her mouth falls open and then she cuts her gaze to me, frowning. "Reed told you about my sketches?"

"I'd love to see them. Do you have them here?"

"They're rough," Lani says, using a reluctant voice that sounds incongruous coming from her.

I spy her sketchbook on the corner of her desk and walk over. "Here's your book, right?"

"Yes, thank you, Reed," she says sharply.

I smile at her. I know it's really none of my business, but I suspect if she didn't get a nudge, she'd never show Nicole a single page.

She flips to a page in the middle, pauses, turns to the next. She scrunches her nose in my direction, then brings the book over to Nicole. "They're nautilus shells. A little more representational than your style."

"Oh." Nicole doesn't say anything else for more than a minute as she studies the drawing, then turns to the next one, which has a few smaller studies of different types of shells. Lani looks at me and bares her teeth. I stick my tongue out at her. She rolls her eyes.

Nicole turns her attention back to us. "You drew these freehand?"

"Yeah. With a mechanical pencil. I have a favorite Japanese model. Really smooth lead."

"Nice," Nicole says. "These would complement the rock series I'm working on. Why don't I scan them in and make some adjustments and I can show you later."

"Really? They're not entirely finished."

"Good enough to start with. You have a really nice eye for detail work. Not surprising, given you're all about the details around here."

"Thanks," Lani mutters, grudgingly accepting the compliment.

"Thank you, Reed. I didn't realize I had another design talent right under my nose."

"You're welcome, Nicole."

"So, dinner? You two, me and Ricky, crab cakes? Or we could go to Mercy SB—oh, wait, they're not open on Mondays. Bummer."

"We're not all going to dinner," Lani says.

"What?" Nicole says with a full-on pout. "Please? I've been eating dehydrated food for three days. The detox unfortunately didn't extend to the food. I want something that doesn't taste like chemicals."

"I'm probably going to be working late, and Reed has to prep for his school thing tomorrow. Right, Reed?"

"I guess. Hey, can I talk to you alone?"

Nicole waves a hand. "I'll go see how things are going up front. Magda was in earlier, so I'm sure Glenn's got his hands full with the order."

"You do that," Lani says, her eyes tracking her sketchbook the entire way. Nicole sets it down on her desk in front of a giant monitor and sashays away.

"So, you met Nicole."

"She's a piece of work. I can see why you like working with her."

"She's a menace," Lani says. "And so are you."

"Must be why you like us both so much." I wiggle my eyebrows and she laughs, despite herself.

"Have you talked to your Realtor?" I ask, returning to the real reason I came to see her.

"Not yet. I'm not sure what I'm going to tell her."

"Well, the offer stands. Please, don't miss out on this opportunity."

"Are you sure? I don't think you've thought this through."

"I have. I'm sure. Look, Lani, you've got dreams, plans. I've got money sitting in the bank, doing nothing. All I do is work, have drinks with Kingston and his friends, with whom I don't have much in common." I wince, realizing I'm turning this into something that's about me and not about her. "The point is, this is something constructive I can do."

She bites her lip. "But I'm going to pay you back."

I do a dorky fist pump on the inside. "No, you're not. The whole point is to avoid more debt, right?"

"Yeah, but—"

"How about this? Whenever I'm in town, you'll put me up in your gorgeous new house. You'll save me a fortune."

"You're already planning to visit?"

"You never know."

She wants to say yes, I can tell. I hold my breath, waiting for her to come to terms with it.

"All right. If this works out, you'll always have a place to stay in Santa Barbara."

"Good enough for me. Now, why can't we go out to dinner with Nicole to celebrate?"

"Because—" She stops. "Honestly, because I don't want to lie to Nicole. I haven't liked lying to any of my friends about you."

"Easy fix. Let's tell them."

"They won't understand. *I* barely understand."

"I know it's unconventional, but they probably know you well enough to expect the unconventional with you from time to time. We'll explain we're exes, and old friends, who happen to also be married to each other, technically."

A gasp makes me turn around. I hadn't heard Nicole come back into the room. She's carrying a large cardboard box and her face is the picture of astonishment. After a beat her consternation dissolves into a smile brighter than a lighthouse beacon. "You two are married?"

CHAPTER 18
LANI

S hit. Shit shit shit shit shit.

Reed, bastard that he is, at least wears a sheepish expression. He knew how much I didn't want to tell Nicole about this. I shoot him my best bitch face and he actually cowers a little. Good. I turn to Nicole, who looks like she's trying not to explode into a million pieces of confetti at this unbelievable news.

"When we were kids, we went to Reno and got married. It was an impulsive decision. Spur of the moment. Spontaneous."

"And other ways to say spontaneous," Reed adds.

I'm going to murder him.

"Then we broke up. Sort of."

"We parted ways," Reed puts in.

I'm getting super irritated with his not-helpful contributions to this conversation.

"Anyway, we stayed married, legally, but until Reed came back to Santa Barbara a few days ago, we hadn't seen each other in over six years."

I can see Nicole processing. She's thinking back through all the years she's known me, analyzing my behavior, thinking about the one-night stands, the flirtations, the vehemence with which I've resisted her matchmaking attempts. She's reading into every single one, trying to make a case for my behavior all being tied back to Reed.

Because when you take all the evidence in at once, it doesn't look good. I look damaged instead of empowered. I look like a girl who is running away from her problems, maybe even pining still for the husband she let get away. For her first love. For—

I suck in a breath. I've got to stop thinking this way.

"Well, now you know," I say, almost defiantly.

"Lani, sweetie, you have to tell the other girls," she says.

My stomach lurches. I know she's right.

"I know," I say quietly. "Fuck."

She puts down the box, comes over and wraps her arm around my shoulders. "Hey, it's going to be fine. They'll understand."

"Will they?" I have the strangest urge to cry. "You don't understand."

"Why, because of your whole Never a Bride pact?" Nicole's voice is soft, but I cringe. She was never supposed to find out about the facetious name for our group of bridesmaids.

"You know about that?"

"I know everything."

Somehow she always does. "You know we weren't trying to hurt your feelings, or leave you out, or anything."

"It's okay. I know from the moment Ricky and I decided to get married I got a little carried away. And you all indulged me because you love me. I loved you for doing it. But I know it wasn't always easy. I figured if you needed that to cope with everything I was throwing at you, then good. I loved seeing the four of you get closer. That's one of the things I'm proudest of from the whole thing."

"Not pulling off the wedding of your dreams? The wedding of the freaking century?"

"That too. But mostly I'm just glad you guys are all still speaking to me. And to each other. And now you need to tell your other Never a Brides what the deal is."

"How?"

"I'll call an emergency meeting. We can go down to Ventura so Rosie doesn't have an excuse for not coming. Dinner, just us girls. Sorry, Reed. Raincheck on the crab cakes?"

"Sure," Reed says. I glare at him. I'm not over the role he's played in this debacle.

"I should have—" I lean my head on Nicole's shoulder so I don't have to look her in the eye. "Well, I should have done a lot of things. But thanks."

"I hate to interrupt, but don't you need to call Beverly?" Reed says.

I jump. "Oh shit. Yes." I almost completely forgot about the other life-changing thing that's happening.

"Why, what's going on?"

"The house I told you about?" I had told Nicole I was looking at houses, in a vague way, but she hasn't heard the latest developments. "They counteroffered, and I'm going to accept."

"That's so exciting!" Nicole is all smiles. "You call Beverly, I'll help Glenn with Magda's order, then make a reservation for tonight. You text O and the others to make sure they'll be there."

"What can I do?" Reed asks.

I scowl at him. "You've done enough," I snap. But then I remember he's giving me twenty-five thousand dollars and relent. Slightly. "I mean it. You're doing a lot for me already."

He doesn't seem perturbed by my hot-cold attitude. "I'm happy to help," he says softly.

I repress the urge to let his tone go right to my heart. Especially not with Nicole as an audience. "Then let us get back to work, okay? I'll text you later."

"You sure?"

I nod. I need space.

"Nicole, it's been a pleasure," he says, bowing slightly in her direction.

"Likewise. Looking forward to seeing you again," she says. "You can go out the back door if you want."

"Oh, I'd like to take another look at something in the front. I'll see myself out." He goes back through the storeroom, taking the weird energy between us with him.

When he's gone, I look at my desk unseeingly. I feel edgy, like I've had one too many cups of coffee. From the emotional rollercoaster that is Nicole finding out what Reed and I are to each other, to the house-buying situation, to the fact that she's looked at my designs and seems to like them, it's a lot.

"Stop thinking and get to work," Nicole says.

She's right. Work will slot everything into place. I dash off a text to the thread, then call Beverly. This is happening. This is my life.

Isn't it fucking great?

> Hi everyone. I'm calling SOS. If there's any way you can get to Ventura for dinner tonight, please come.

ROSIE

> You're coming to my neck of the woods? Awesome. I should be able to get off work by 6.

> Perfect thanks

> BTW, Nicole's coming. And she knows about the Never a Bride thing.

OPHELIA

> Wait, seriously? I thought we'd kept that pretty locked down.

She says she knows everything

OPHELIA

Well, that's true

ROSIE

Gotta run, but I'll see you tonight

OPHELIA

What's the emergency? I was going to watch Outlander with Jamie (ha!) tonight, but we could put it off.

I'd rather tell you when we're all together.

OPHELIA

Is Reed coming?

No. Girls only, please.

OPHELIA

Just wondering. He confirmed with me for tomorrow, so I know he's still in town.

Yes, he's still in town. No, he's not coming to dinner.

OPHELIA

OK

KATE

Hey ladies! Got room for one more? One and a half if you count the Bean.

OPHELIA

Kate!!

Are you back?

KATE

Oliver had some restaurant emergency, so we came back last night. I'm in Camarillo right now, so dinner is doable.

Great! Can't wait to see you and hear all about NYC

OPHELIA

Yay!

KATE

How does Nicole know about the NABs? Is she mad?

I don't know

But no. She's cool.

OPHELIA

It's not like she's not laughing her way to the bank, considering three out of four of us are the next best thing to married

Gotta go! See you tonight!

CHAPTER 19

LANI

The restaurant Nicole has chosen is stylish but not fussy, and the five of us arrive nearly at the same time, so we get in plenty of hugs and kisses and exclamations of delighted surprise at how big Kate's belly has gotten in the scant weeks since we've seen her last.

"How many weeks is it now?" I ask as we sit down at a cozy table in a corner of the restaurant.

"About twenty-five," Kate says, exuding maternal glow from every single pore, like she has since the minute she found out she was pregnant.

"I never understood why pregnancies are measured in weeks." Ophelia grabs a piece of bread from the center of the table and slathers it with butter. "We don't measure anything else in weeks."

"Maybe to give you the illusion of having more time than you really do before you've got a helpless infant to take care of?" Kate suggests.

"Tell us everything about New York," Nicole demands. It's a round table so no one is technically at the head, but Nicole seems like King Arthur anyway.

"It was amazing! Oliver was so adorable. Best tour guide I

could ask for. We saw four Broadway shows, tried a dozen restaurants. His parents were really sweet. We stayed with them, but it wasn't weird. They have a really active life, so we barely saw them. I think they're so happy Oliver's in a relationship that's lasted longer than three days, and they're going to be grandparents again. Aziza wants to come out and help when the baby's born, but I can see us moving there someday."

That declaration is met by complete silence.

"What?" Kate looks around the table. "Not anytime soon, but you know that's where Oliver's family is, and I've always secretly wanted to live there, so…"

"I think that's great," Ophelia says, breaking our speechlessness. "I can totally see you all glamorous and New York-y. Oliver will open the hottest restaurant in town, and you'll shake up the East Coast podcast scene. Is that a thing?"

"Thanks, O. And if we do, you know you gals will always have someplace to crash when you come visit."

"Sounds perfect. Maybe Lani will have a reason to go there sooner than later." This from Nicole, who has shown admirable restraint in bringing up my dirty laundry so far.

"Why's that?" Kate asks, right on cue.

"You haven't been here, so you haven't met Reed!" Rosie says, clapping her hands together. "I'm so pumped I know something before Kate."

"Who's Reed?"

Ophelia puts on her librarian hat. "Reed Bennet is the acclaimed author of a terrific series of picture books. He's coming to my school tomorrow to do a reading. The kids are going to go wild."

"And he's an old friend of Lani's from college," Rosie adds. "We all got to meet him last night—except Nicole. He got along great with the menfolk. Gus really liked him. It's too bad he lives so far away—the Bronx?"

"Queens, actually," Nicole says. "He came into the shop today so I got to meet him, too. Interesting guy."

"Wow, you all seem very taken with this celebrity author friend of Lani's. I'm sorry I missed all the excitement," Kate says.

"Yes, so that's why I wanted to see you tonight. I need to tell you…" Why is this so difficult? "Look, I haven't been entirely open with you about something. And it's way past time I told you, and I hope you guys can forgive me."

"What is it, Lani?" Ophelia asks. She's sitting next to me and puts her bread down in order to put her hand on my shoulder.

I look at Nicole, who nods encouragingly.

"So I know we started our Never a Bride group to help us through all the bridesmaid craziness—no offense, Nicole."

"None taken." She shrugs carelessly, belying all those months of bridal nonsense.

"That might have been a good time to tell you that, um, I'm married. To Reed."

A silence descends much like the one after Kate said she might move to New York. I rush to fill it with words. "But only on paper. And I didn't think it mattered because that part of my life was so long ago. But then he showed up here and started charming the pants off all of you and I didn't want to lie, but I also didn't want to be the weird girl with the secret husband, so I let you believe he was an old friend, ex, whatever. Which isn't not true but…I'm sorry."

I force myself to look at the faces of the closest girlfriends I've ever had, bracing myself for expressions of betrayal or disgust. Nicole looks like her usual self while the rest of them just look surprised.

"You don't have to be sorry," Rosie says finally. "You had your reasons. You don't owe us anything."

"I didn't mean to keep such a big secret from you, but I guess I've always felt like the most expendable member of this group, and if I didn't qualify as a Never a Bride, that would keep me even more on the outside."

"What are you talking about? You're not expendable." This from Nicole.

I wave my hands in the air. This is a conversation I've had with myself a dozen times. "I'm not family, like Ophelia. I haven't known you since college, like Kate and Rosie. I wouldn't even be a part of this crew if I didn't work with you. Not to mention I'm not white, I sleep around, I drive a car from the sixties. I'm different."

"Is that how you really feel?" Kate looks pained.

I sigh. "Not exactly. I know the friendships I have with each of you are real. It's just...I don't know." The relationships I have with these four women are the most important friendships of my life, and in my experience the more you love something, the easier it is for it to disappear.

"You are different, Lani. That's a good thing. And honestly, it's kind of a relief to know that you aren't a perfect ice queen who is okay with all of her life choices all the time," Ophelia says in her quietly devastating way.

Rosie nods enthusiastically at that statement.

"I'm not an ice queen," I protest.

"We know you're not, because we're your friends, to whom you are very important, and without whom we would be lesser people," Kate says deliberately. "But you're such a boss all the time. You run Winesap Design, plus you have a social life and you look like a million dollars every single damn day. You can cook while lord knows the rest of us can barely boil water. You're a little bit intimidating, when even your friends think your life is like an Instagram post come to life."

"Turns out I'm more like a reality TV show—absent husband and keeping secrets from my best friends," I say grumpily. "Which I'm sorry about, again, for the record."

"We know you are," Rosie says kindly.

"I think I thought if I wasn't perfect, you guys wouldn't like me as much."

"That's nonsense. We like you for lots of reasons, but you not being perfect? Both a relief and old news," Nicole says dryly.

I laugh. "It is?"

"Yeah, you're sarcastic and you have super high standards and you work too hard and—"

"Okay, okay, I get the picture," I say. "Well, glad that's all cleared up. Thanks for being so understanding." My heart is full with love for these four women.

"Of course, honey," Nicole says. "But the real question is, what's going on with you and Reed?"

"Fuck me," I groan. "You convinced me to come clean and bare my insecurities, and now you want to grill me on this?"

"Of course! I mean, there's got to be a reason why you stayed married. You're the least lazy person I know, so it's not like you just didn't get around to filing the paperwork. Please spill." Ophelia looks at me expectantly, and since she's the one I lied to most egregiously, I cave.

"I need wine. Then I will tell you what I know, which, believe me, isn't much."

"Deal."

We take a break to order food and glasses of wine, rather than bottles, since we're driving and Kate can't imbibe. Once I'm fortified with a healthy slug of California pinot and have devoured my portion of bruschetta, I open my mouth to explain. Nothing comes out.

I don't know what to say. So I say that.

"Well, tell us how you met. Was he that hot in college?" Nicole asks, chin in her hands as if anticipating a really juicy story.

"You think he's hot?" I've always been attracted to him, but he's not your typical pretty boy.

Rosie chimes in. "I have to admit to noticing the way he fills out his shirts. Solid, dependable. Like a pickup truck."

"He wasn't built like that when we first met, he was a few inches shorter, baby fat, baby face. He was a baby, full stop. A freshman. I was a junior. We were in a film class together and halfway through fall semester he asked me out."

"That's ballsy for a freshman, right?" Kate asks.

"I thought so. I turned him down flat."

"So what changed? How did you end up marrying the baby film student?"

I cover my face with my hands. "Ugh, this is why I didn't tell you. It messes with my image so much."

"Your image will recover," Kate says.

"Fine, fine. Well, I refused to date him, but somehow we became friends. Even though I was all about business and Econ, most of my friends were theater or English majors, like Reed, and he fit right in with them."

"Friends first. Makes sense," Ophelia says, having fallen victim to that storyline herself.

"Well, friendly hanging out somehow turned into kissing and that turned into sex and then we were just...together. I'd never had a long-term boyfriend before. And it wasn't how I thought it would be, being in a relationship. I'd seen my friends have drama and fights and tears, and it wasn't like that with Reed. We never let each other off easy, maybe, but we also just vibed."

"So how did you end up married?" Rosie asks.

"He'd applied to some grad programs but couldn't afford any of them, so he was at loose ends, and I was in between semesters on my MBA. One day he said, 'Let's go on a road trip.' We'd do that—pack a bag and take off on the spur of the moment. Once we drove all night so we could watch the sun rise in Joshua Tree. We always had so much fun."

I smile, remembering those trips, bickering over music and

gorging ourselves on gas station snacks, hopped up on candy and soda.

"We were halfway to Tahoe when he said, 'Let's go all the way to Reno and get married.' I thought he was crazy, but also, you know, I loved him. In the years we'd been together I'd never once thought about us breaking up. So we did it, giddy and young and so stupid because we were happy."

I remember I couldn't stop smiling or touching my cheap gold wedding band, too wrapped up in Reed and feeling like my adult life was really starting.

"A week later, he got a call from this really prestigious, practically free MFA program in Iowa. He'd gotten in off the waitlist. And he said he was going. He obviously expected I'd drop everything and go with him, especially now that we were married. But I liked Santa Barbara, I liked my job and my MBA program. He didn't have anything tying him here, except me. And I get that this was an important opportunity and I didn't not want him to go, but I didn't expect him to give me an ultimatum.

"His parents weren't supportive of his dream to be a writer. When they cut him off, he cut them out of his life. He did the same thing with me. I wouldn't come with him, and he wouldn't compromise, and he left, and we barely spoke again after that."

"Jesus." The girls all look stricken, and we're all unsettled when the perky server arrives to distribute our meals.

"Yeah. Wow. I've never laid it all out there like that before," I say, stabbing a tomato with my fork. "Sorry to be such a downer."

"It sounds like you made a good couple. But you were young. And people sometimes grow apart," Nicole says.

"In this case, we grew apart because he planted himself thousands of miles away."

"Do you think you would have done anything differently if you had to do it over?" Rosie asks softly.

That is a question I've posed to myself a thousand times. "When he left, he broke my heart. But could I have been more flexible? Tried to make it work long distance? I don't know. Probably.

"Then again, not having a guy around while I established my career actually helped. How do you think I get so much done at the office, Nicole? It's because I don't have someone waiting on me at the end of the day. And I know Reed's changed a lot in these years. He's grown up in a way he wouldn't have if he'd stayed here. Stayed with me. I think he's had a rough time overall, but it's made him stronger. I'm proud of him."

"Wow, Lani, I take it back. You are fucking perfect. You're so generous, even to the guy who broke your heart. You want the best for him, it's clear. You still care about him," Nicole says.

"Yeah." No point in lying about it. "I do. I thought there wasn't anything left between us. The old Lani and Reed, the ones who were married for like five minutes, they're dead. But real-life Reed and Lani, who are getting to know each other again? I think there might be something there."

"I knew it," Nicole says, triumphant. "The way he looks at you!" She pantomimes a swoon.

"What?" My cheeks feel prickly with heat. "How does he look at me?"

"I've seen it, too," Ophelia says. "Like you invented the undo command. In awe of your brilliance and stunning good looks. Which is every guy, honestly."

"I've noticed it, too," Rosie says. "It's like every time he looks at you, he's surprised you're still there. Like he's pinching himself to be in the same room as you."

I don't know what to do with that. Somehow telling them he's giving me thousands of dollars seems like a bad idea, but

I'm done with secrets and lying. "There's something else. I'm buying a house. I just accepted the counteroffer from the sellers."

I accept the eruption of congratulations and exclamations of surprise. "What's the address?" Kate pulls out her phone. "I'll Zillow it."

I hold up a finger at her to wait a minute. "But in the interest of not keeping things from you and since it's sort of on point, you should know I didn't want to meet the counteroffer at first, even though I'm fully in love with this house, because it would have left me in a bind with the repairs I want to do. House rich, cash poor. But Reed offered to make up the difference and I took him up on it. Do you think that's a huge mistake?"

"Wow. That's what you guys were talking about at the shop this afternoon, isn't it?" Nicole says. She actually does know everything.

"Yes."

"You know, Lani, I would have been happy to work something out with you if I'd known you needed help. A loan or an advance. We've been meaning to renegotiate the profit-sharing clause of your contract."

"I do know that. Really." Nicole has never not been there for me. For any of us.

She goes on. "But I know you wouldn't have wanted to ask. I admire your independence, but you accepting help from Reed —well, I think it's great. Great that you would listen to him and recognize that he wants to help, and let yourself accept that help."

I hadn't thought of it in those terms. Could I be exhibiting some of the flexibility I wasn't able to show Reed when he left?

"You couldn't be more wrong when you say you're the most expendable member of this group. You've made my life immeasurably better since I met you. You make coming to work every day a joy. Hell, without you, I'd probably be hand-stitching throw pillows in my living room and giving them away as Christmas presents. I owe you so much. And you're tied for first as the coolest woman I know." She pauses and looks around the table at each of her bridesmaids, friends, sisters.

"But it's only today that I feel like I'm starting to know the real Lani, the one who sometimes makes decisions based on her heart, not her head. The one who's had her heart broken. The one who freaking draws like a botanical engineer. Did you all know Lani sketches? Her shells are going to be featured in next summer's line. So all I can say is, please, don't leave us. We love you. We need you. And we'll always want you around, no matter if it turns out you have five husbands in different states."

The joke stops me from completely breaking down in tears. I make a face. "God forbid. I can barely manage one estranged husband."

Everyone giggles, tension from Nicole's grand speech dispelled.

"I love you all, too, you know."

"We know," Kate says, leaning over to rub my shoulder. "I'm so lucky this baby is going to have so many cool aunts."

With friends like these, who needs anything else, truly. That's the real meaning of the Never a Brides. It's not that we were bitter man-haters who were curdled to societal expectations. Well, maybe five percent of it was that. We knew the four of us, and Nicole, too, were more valuable to each other than the next guy who might or might not stick around. We created a space for our sisterhood to be about something else—our work, our dreams, our fears.

Even if Kate moves away, or if Rosie and Gus end up having kids, or if Ophelia and Jamie finally move into together, or if I get my dream house and conquer the world, we'll always be a family, no matter what.

CHAPTER 20

REED

Heart emoji? What the fuck? I sort of answered on autopilot, glad she agreed to see me, but now I stare at the little red heart as if I can erase it with the power of my mind. Lani is not a heart emoji kind of person. When she doesn't immediately text me back that lunch is off due to inappropriate emoji use, I relax somewhat, clicking off my phone and grabbing my copy of *Reed and Lucy Go to the Movies* in case the box of books I asked Kingston to overnight to Ophelia's school hasn't made it.

I'm looking forward to my first appearance in front of a crowd. I've got another one this afternoon at a local bookstore, and two tomorrow. It'll be good to stay busy. I was bored out of my mind last night with Lani off spending time with her friends and not knowing anyone else in the area. I'd considered texting Ophelia's boyfriend Jamie to see if he wanted to hang out, but Lani might think I'm insinuating myself too far into her life, and I don't want to make things awkward.

Especially since things have been going kind of well. The more time I spend with Lani, the more I learn about the tremendous life she's created for herself here, I have absolutely no desire to go back to lonely, dirty, depressing New York when I could be here in sunny Southern California with the most incredible woman I've ever known.

It's a short walk to the school. I arrive early, pass through security, and meet Ophelia at the door of her domain. Her library is small and organized, like her.

"Thanks for coming, Reed. The kids are so excited. The first graders are coming in a few minutes. And thank you so much for the books! Your publisher overnighted ten copies of the entire series. So generous. I'll have plenty for the library and can also send some of the kids home with their own copies. Plus, I was hoping you might sign a set that I could put in the school's silent auction fundraiser."

"Of course." I'm glad my publisher didn't cheap out on this. "Is that a 3D printer?"

"Yes, we have our own maker lab right in the library. We were a pilot school, but Jamie and I are in the process of installing one of these in every school in the district. We should be up and running everywhere by Thanksgiving."

"So cool." Ophelia gives me a quick tour of the rest of the library. It smells like books and industrial carpeting, and the combination of scents is oddly comforting. I meet Ingrid, the assistant librarian who helps corral the students when they file in and take their seats on the carpet in front of a couple of straight-backed school chairs.

I have a quick flash of nerves—there's no reason this book won't be well-received, but there's always something a bit nerve-wracking about presenting my work to the target audience, no filter, nothing protecting me from their reactions.

Ophelia introduces me briefly, and I stare into the sea of small faces, all looking up at me expectantly. My breathing goes shallow. I didn't think this was going to be so hard. Then I see a little girl who reminds me of Lani, the same fall of black hair and similarly determined eyes. She's Lucy. She deserves to see a story with someone like her in it. I clear my throat and start to read.

What feels like an age later, but is more likely about seven minutes, the kids are clapping and laughing, and Ophelia is beaming. My palms are sweaty, but I think it went well.

"Does anyone have a question for Mr. Bennet?" Ophelia asks. She calls on a freckle-faced boy with red hair. "Andres?"

"Are you the Reed in the book?"

I get that a lot. "Sort of. Reed in the book is a version of me. He's his own character, but we're similar."

"So do you have a friend named Lucy?"

I smile. Common follow-up question. Kids are smart. "I don't, but I have a friend named Lani, and she's a lot like Lucy."

"Does she like movies?"

"She does." I think about all those movie nights we had back in college, about how we met in a film class. Suddenly, more than anything, I want a chance to watch a movie with Lani again. We could talk and snark and chat through the whole thing and it would be super fun. And if the movie turns out to be terrible, we could let it play in the background while we make out until the credits interrupt us.

Uh, time to course correct. I don't need to be thinking about making out at an elementary school.

Ophelia gets them to ask a few more questions, which I try to answer as honestly as possible. "Okay, last one. Candace?"

It's the girl who reminds me of Lani. I mean, Lucy.

"How do you become a writer? I like to make up stories, but my mom says writers don't make any money."

"Well, some writers don't make very much compared to the amount of work it takes to write something like a book, but there are lots of kinds of writers, people who write articles for magazines and newspapers, people who write the books you read in school, people who write books for grown-ups, and people who write books for children."

"Like you," Candace observes.

"Right, like me. I'm a children's book author and illustrator. And it's not the kind of writer I thought I would become, but it's the best job in the world. Because I get to think of stories and draw lots of pictures and then I get to share those stories and pictures with people like you. And sometimes I make you laugh and sometimes I make you think, and that's pretty special. And if any of you think you'd like to write stories someday, I want you to try. The world will always need storytellers. The world is going to need your stories. And you're the only one who can tell stories like you. Cool how that works."

Ophelia's eyes are bright when she wraps up the session, dismissing each class in turn back to their classroom.

"That was fun," I say when it's just Ophelia and Ingrid and me in the suddenly quiet space. "Successful first stop on the *Reed and Lucy Go to the Movies* West Coast book tour. Tough crowd, but I think it went over."

"Are you kidding?" Ingrid says. "They were hanging on your every word. I think you really got through to some of them about thinking about writing. That was really inspired, Reed. You're great with kids."

"I'm an overgrown kid myself, so," I say, a touch embarrassed at the praise.

"You have lunch plans?" Ophelia asks. "I can take my break a little early if you want. There's a park Jamie and I meet for lunch at that's not far. Ocean views."

"Tempting, but I'm going to bring Lani something at work."

Her smile turns steely when I mention Lani. "Oh? That's nice. You know, Lani's one of my best friends."

"Awesome."

"It's great you guys are reconnecting, but…"

I have the sense I'm about to be dressed down by a five-foot-nothing children's librarian. Appropriate. "Go on, let me have it."

"I know you two have a…complicated history. And Lani's a tough cookie, but she's quick to forgive, generous, loyal. She also has a slight issue with making herself an island so people can't get to her, and that doesn't always work out. You have to know this is hard for her, having you suddenly back in her life."

I choose my words carefully. "I know I've caused her pain in the past. I definitely never want to do that again."

"Really? Then you'd better be really careful. Because I think you have a unique power to hurt her and maybe you don't even realize it."

"No one can make Lani think or feel anything," I say, a bit stubbornly. "She makes her own choices."

"True. But she might feel like she has to make a choice to protect herself if you won't do it for her."

What does that mean? "I don't know if that's up to me."

I can tell Ophelia is getting impatient with me when she starts pacing. I take a defensive step back.

"Look, you live on the other side of the country. You're only here for a few days. You're lending, giving, her money, whatever, like a knight in shining armor, and you essentially write a love letter to her every six months when you publish another Reed and Lucy book. It's clear there's unfinished business, but it's not clear what you want or what you're doing with my girl, and I want you to know that as much as I like you, Reed Bennet, you're on notice with me, and with the other girls. Lani's our family and we're going to protect her, even if you won't."

I vaguely register that Ingrid has tried to make herself invisible in the graphic novel section while I take my medicine. Ophelia looks like a good witch from a fairy tale, with her shining eyes and golden hair, self-righteously beautiful. I'm strangely happy to be so passionately told off. It means that Lani has friends who will stand up for her no matter the cost.

"I'm glad she has you." I mess with the leather strap around my wrist as I figure out how to put this into words. "And you're right that things are complicated. I don't claim to have it all figured out. I barely know what I'm doing half the time. With Lani, I act on instinct because she's a fundamental part of me. I'll always feel that way about her. We have a lot of history. I guess what I didn't know until I got here and saw her again was if we had any future. I still can't answer that question, but I hear your warning loud and clear, and all I can say is I promise to do my best. I don't want to hurt her any more than I already have."

"Well, good." She seems to relent a bit. "Lani's my priority, but you know, if you ever need anything, I guess you can call on us, me and Rosie and Nicole. Kate, too, though she only knows you by reputation at this point, but I'm sure you'll meet her before long. Lani's birthday is coming up and we're all planning to have dinner at Oliver's restaurant. Will you be around?"

I feel a stab of longing so sharp I almost gasp. I want this so badly. I want this to be my life. Friends and dinners and casual offers for help and a found family. The only friends I have in New York are those people with whom I have financial entanglements, my editor, my roommates, even Erin—she works for the publisher who pays my bills. I basically pay Kingston to be friends with me, being my agent and all.

"I'd love to be there," I say, my voice slightly hoarse. "If Lani's okay with it." How do I separate my longing to be part of this world with my longing for her?

CHAPTER 21
LANI

My Tuesday morning is completely bananas, not least because I woke up with a slight emotional hangover after last night's Never-a-Bride lovefest. I'm rushing around my office, trying to fit in as much work as I can before Reed shows up with lunch. I look up when the stockroom door opens, but it's only Glenn bringing me a manila envelope.

I recognize my Realtor's return address and slide open the flap. It's the binder for the house, with the agreed-upon price. The actual amount of money involved is kind of mind-boggling. No one in my family has ever owned their own house.

Growing up working class on Kauai we rented a series of apartments while my mom worked for the county. Good benefits, flexible schedule for her to raise my sister and me. It was a perfectly fine existence, except for the glaring hole that was my father leaving us. I was eight, Akela was five. Handsome and charming, he and my mom got together young and they fought all the time, and then one day he was loading up the trunk of his car, that beat-up BMW 2002 that I'm pretty sure he loved more than us.

You wouldn't think it would be easy for someone to

abandon their children when they lived on a 550-square-mile island, but I only saw him a handful of times after that. I was in middle school when he dropped dead from an embolism.

I never got a chance to find out if we might someday have a different relationship.

I stare at the contract. It's a ton of money and a huge responsibility. I'm banking that I'll be able to afford the mortgage and the taxes and the insurance and all of those pesky grown-up things. That I'll keep making the same kind of money I'm making now, maybe even more. That I can handle this.

I've lived in Santa Barbara for twelve years. I've never wanted to move back to Hawaii. It's a nice place to visit, but this is my home now. Putting down roots here feels right. And it even feels right that Reed is a little bit tied up in it all. It's not like I'm going to be thinking of him every time I come home, but I'd like to think his spirit, the part of him that encouraged me and pushed me to ask for more than I might have otherwise, will be present in the house.

And if he's serious, then he'll be there physically once in a while, too. I'm not sure what would bring him back when he hasn't had a reason to come for over half a decade, but I'd like to think I'd be a good enough reason, now that we're friends again.

I'm reading the contract when the storeroom door opens again, and this time Reed steps through. He's wearing his standard uniform of jeans and a T-shirt, plus a baseball cap and a flannel overshirt tied around his waist. He carries an enormous brown paper bag that I hope has something yummy inside.

"Great timing. I'm starving."

"And hello to you, too," he says, smiling.

I'm brusque to cover up how happy I am to see him. "I've had a super busy day and breakfast was a protein bar."

"Ophelia told me about this place that has really good cookies, so I went there."

"If O recommended it, you better believe the cookies will be good." I peer into the bag and see sandwiches and a couple of sides, and my mouth starts watering. "Gimme."

"Whatcha doing?" he asks as he starts unloading everything onto the desk.

"Got the paperwork on the house. I have to sign and return it with a check today."

"Everything look good?"

"So far. I can't believe I'm about to spend this much money on a place to live."

"Real estate is a good investment. You'll be building equity. Plus, no more annoying neighbors. Or at least, no annoying neighbors you have to share a wall with."

I laugh. "I know, you don't have to sell me on homeownership. I'm excited. It's just a big step. But one I think I'm ready for."

"Congratulations, Lani. I'm really proud of you."

"Thanks. And thanks for your help. You gave me the push I needed to not let this fall through my fingers."

"I'm happy I could help."

We spend a few minutes eating, and then I remember to ask, "How did it go at the school today?"

"It was really good. Slightly terrifying. Nothing like reading your own fiction out loud to a hostile public. But they seemed to like it."

"I haven't read the new book," I say. "I think my favorite so far is the first one."

"You're not alone. I think one of the reviews of this latest one said something like, 'Bennet continues to chase the magic of the first in the series, with middling results.'"

"Ouch."

He shrugs. "They're not wrong. That's one of the reasons Kingston wanted me to come out here. He thought I might find some inspiration."

"How's that working out for you?"

He eyes me. "I would say certain aspects of this trip have been very inspiring. And I've filled myself with amazing food, that's for sure."

"New York has good food, too, right?"

"Sure, if you're rich. For a long time I subsisted on crappy weak coffee, dry falafel, and greasy pizza."

"You really don't like it there, huh."

"I'm definitely going to be moving in the near future."

"Anyplace in particular or just anyplace but there?" I control my voice so it doesn't sound like I'm too invested in the answer.

"I've been considering my options," he says lightly. "I'm renting a car tomorrow and driving to L.A. I have a bunch of readings the next couple of days, but I should be back here by Friday."

So he's going to L.A. for a couple of days. I have a ton of work to do. I can do without the distraction. But I still feel a little weird, like if he drives away from Santa Barbara, away from me, I won't see him again for another six years.

"I'm supposed to head back east on Saturday, but I could push my flight. If I stick around for a while, can I see you? I know you're busy and I don't want to take up all your time. I've got to work on the new draft if I'm going to make my deadline. But I thought if you wanted to...because I want to. Obviously."

I'm a little confused. "If I wanted to what?"

"Go out with me? Like a date."

"*Like* a date?"

"A date. A real date. Me taking you out someplace you like and eating and talking and finding out if we could be...if we feel...well, finding out how we feel."

"Sounds like a pretty high-stakes date."

He backpedals so fast his tires start to smoke. "No! No stakes. Low pressure. You know, casual."

I can't help but laugh, even though it's with an edge of despair. "It has been surprisingly fun to hang out with you this week. And if this time has shown me anything, it's that you're still a good friend." I take a moment to collect my thoughts. "Do you think dating is a good idea?"

"No, totally, you're right," he says. "I'm getting ahead of myself. I didn't mean to pressure you. I'm just...I wanted to say that I've been happy here this week. And I know I'm a selfish bastard, but I like that happy feeling. I want more of it. But that's not on you."

"I think if you're unhappy in New York you should change your situation," I say. "But you can't construct your happiness around me. I may not know much about functional relationships, but I know that's a recipe for disaster."

He looks like a little boy who didn't get the bike he wanted for Christmas. Not my problem, I remind myself. I'm not his mom.

"These cookies are really good," I say. "Macadamia nut is my favorite."

"I know," he says softly. "You were the one who turned me onto them."

His crooked smile makes my skin feel prickly. I glance away and note the time. "I've got a conference call in a few minutes. Thanks for lunch." I wince a little at how stilted my dismissal is.

He stands up, starts gathering our trash. "I've got to get to my next reading."

"Hey, you have plans after? I have a bunch of produce in my fridge that needs to get eaten. You should come over and have dinner. As friends."

"Are you sure?"

No. "Please. Six?"

"Want me to bring anything?"

"Um, how about a copy of *Reed and Lucy Go to the Movies*?"

"I'll get it signed by the author for you." He winks and I feel oddly bereft even though he's right there.

What the hell am I doing?

CHAPTER 22

REED

The second reading of the day isn't as much fun as the first. The audience is mostly parents with kids younger than the ones at Ophelia's school, and their questions are repetitive, but the independent bookshop is thrilled with the number of copies we sell. My hand cramps up from scribbling my name over and over.

After, I browse the shelves and pick up a couple of titles I've been meaning to read. I read a lot on my phone's e-reader apps but will always love the reassuring weight of a book in my hands.

When I get back to my rental I pack my stuff, since I'll be leaving tomorrow for a hotel in L.A. I take a shower and change into my last set of clean clothes. I'd had some idea of finding a laundromat somewhere on my journey; I probably should have figured that out before now. I eye my suitcase, mostly filled with dirty clothes, then the slim brown paper package sitting on my bed. I take one last look at myself in the mirror. I've definitely got five o'clock shadow, but it's too late to shave. Besides, this isn't a date. I botched that spectacularly earlier, but at least Lani's making me a pity dinner.

Lunch had been painful, longing for Lani while she kept

herself just out of my reach. It's becoming clear I want more than I can have. Then again, Lani is giving me the very great gift of her friendship.

I'll have to make it be enough.

Change your situation, she said to me. Good advice. Maybe I need to get my shit together before I'd be any good as a boyfriend anyway. Weird to consider myself boyfriend material for the woman who is technically my wife.

I order a ride, grab my suitcase, backpack, and the package. As long as we're talking, as long as we're friends, there's always a chance we could be something more. I'm not saying I deserve it, but I know now that I definitely want it.

The drive feels like it takes an hour in the tail end of rush hour, even though it's probably only fifteen minutes. I text Lani to let her know I'm there and she buzzes open the downstairs door.

"Moving in?" she asks when she sees my suitcase.

I grimace. "Not exactly. I was actually hoping to ask for a huge favor. Can I do a load of laundry in your machine?"

Her face freezes for a second, and then she's doubled over laughing, no, *cackling*.

"What's so funny?"

"You haven't changed a bit, Reed Bennet." She's smiling as she says it, so I guess that's not a bad thing. "And yes, you can use my washing machine. I'm getting dinner going. You can put your clothes in and then open up some wine."

"Thanks."

She points out the little stacked washer-dryer combo in a closet in the hallway.

"Please tell me you don't need my help," she says, still laughing a little.

"I do know how to do laundry, for your information." But I kind of get her point. Growing up, my stay-at-home mom's mission in life was running the household affairs of my father, who worked super long hours at his construction company, and me and my brothers' and sister's lives. She didn't teach us how to do laundry. I went to college not being able to fold so much as a beach towel. It's not my mom's fault I was hopelessly dependent on her, but my learning curve was slow. It wasn't until Lani and I started living together that I figured out how to do basic tasks like load a dishwasher and take out the recycling.

"I think you'd be surprised at how domesticated I am now," I call in the direction of the kitchen as I locate the soap, something lavender and organic, and measure an appropriate amount into the machine, then layer my jeans, T-shirts, and boxers. I select the cycle carefully, refusing to fail this test.

"I'm sure I would be," Lani calls back.

I leave the suitcase in the hall, bringing the package, which I set on the bar before heading to the little fridge where Lani keeps her wine. Her apartment feels familiar by now. I wish I didn't have to go to L.A. tomorrow, but Kingston will kill me if I back out, not to mention that I can't disappoint the bookstores or the kids who are planning to come see me.

"Red or white?"

"How about white? I'm making fish."

I survey the bottles. I'm no expert, but I grab one with a nice label and set about opening it.

As the wine glugs into the glass, I realize I'm stalling. "I brought you a present," I say, handing her the wine and the package.

She stops shredding kale, wipes her hands on a dishtowel, and takes both.

"It feels like a book," she says, weighing it, then tears the paper open. Inside is a copy of *Reed and Lucy Go to the Movies.* And something else. She holds up the narrow object, also wrapped in brown paper. "What's this?"

"Part of the present. You could consider it an early birthday gift, I guess. Or, since you aren't a huge fan of your birthday, just a general thanks-for-being-you present." I force myself to stop babbling and take a too-big sip of wine.

She gets the paper open and the gold chain with the cat's-eye pendant settles into her cupped palm. She inspects it, then glances up at me. "Wait, this is from the store."

"Yep. I saw it and it made me think of you."

"Wow, I love this designer's style. This is gorgeous. Thank you."

"You like it? Because I could probably exchange it. I have an in at the place I got it."

She gives me a look as if she's trying not to laugh at my dad-quality joke. "Ha ha. Help me put it on?"

I walk around the kitchen bar and take the chain from her. She lifts her silky hair away from the nape of her neck. I want to kiss the curve where her neck meets her shoulder and nip at the shell of her ear. I want to press myself against the length of her back and rock into her, crowd her against the counter. Fuck dinner. Fuck wine.

I only want her.

I clear my throat and unhook the chain's clasp with unsteady fingers. It takes me a couple of tries to thread it, but then the pendant falls against her sternum and she turns around, not enough inches between us. I keep my eyes on the jewelry, which looks at home against her light brown skin. "Pretty."

"Thanks, Reed."

I'm about to step back, out of the realm of temptation, but her arms come up around my neck and she's kissing me, hot and open-mouthed. I groan and kiss back.

This is not a "thanks for the pretty necklace" kiss or a "isn't it great we're friends again" kiss. This is the kiss of someone who wants to get laid.

I want so much more than that, but I'm willing to take what I can get.

I bunch my hands up in her shirt, rucking it up out of her skirt, skimming my fingers along the bare skin of her waist and pulling her as close to me as possible. She bends her back, arching into me, and it's like my fantasy come to life as I press her into the counter, boxing her in with my legs. She goes with it, letting me move her and touch her and kiss her feverishly over her mouth, along her jaw, down to the curve of her neck I'd just been coveting. Now I have it. I kiss the exposed skin, then lick it, then bite it softly.

Lani gasps, squeezes my arms. "Reed."

I pull myself away from her reluctantly. "Yeah?"

"What are we doing?"

"Um." Is this a trick question?

"I'm sorry I kissed you without asking."

"It's okay." I guess I lost some brain cells when she kissed the breath out of me, or maybe it's that all the blood from my head has recently traveled south, because I feel immensely stupid.

"I should finish making dinner," she says quietly.

"All right." My vision focuses. She's gorgeous, lips kissed pink and plump, outfit mussed, hair flying every which way. "I should take you to bed."

"What?"

"I mean, I want to take you to bed. But you want to make dinner. So that's what we'll do. I can, um, chop something."

"Reed?"

"Yes?"

"I changed my mind. Take me to bed."

CHAPTER 23

LANI

Reed wastes no time acting on my request. He picks me up, bridal style, ironically enough, and carries me to the bedroom.

I know I started this, and I know I can stop it at any time, but I really, really don't want to. It hasn't been that long since I had sex, a few weeks at most—the guy I met at the farmers market with the cute puppy that I'm almost entirely sure he got to help him pick up women—but it's been a long time since I had sex with someone I care about and can have a conversation with beyond platitudes.

Reed is nothing like the hookups and with-benefits situations I have. He knows me. I know him. I tremble in his arms.

My room is a bit of a mess—I was in a rush this morning, didn't bother to make the bed—and he lays me down in the bunched-up sheets carefully, like setting a glass egg down in tissue paper. The room is cool and goosebumps prick my skin. I'm extra sensitive all over and he's not even touching me right now.

No, Reed is stripping off his T-shirt, exposing the broad expanse of his chest. He's not *Men's Health* cut, but he's lost the baby fat I used to cuddle against and find so comforting. The dusting of light brown hair between his pecs is new to me, as well. We were really such kids when we first got together. But the person standing at the foot of my bed, with his chin covered in stubble, the leather strap on his wrist accentuating the thickness of his arm muscles, currently undoing the buttons of his fly, is all man.

"You're so fucking sexy, Lani," he says, startling me out of my blatant perusal of his body. He leaves his fly undone enough that I can see the outline of his erection straining the fabric of his boxers, but then he sits down on the bed and leans over to take off his boots.

I wonder if I should take off my clothes, too, since Reed seems really focused on getting naked, but before I can get my fingers on the zipper of my skirt, he stands back up, slides his jeans and boxers off in one motion and my mouth waters at the sight of him, large, thick, cut, springing up from a neat brown thatch of hair.

"You're gorgeous, too." It comes out without my permission. My bedroom talk usually consists of lightly dirty encouragement and some gentle direction when needed, but that's because I've rarely known my partners for more than a few hours. We're there to get each other off, to have fun—it's not a trust exercise. But Reed, even though he has hurt me more than any other man, I do trust. He's a decent person, a good human. And he has a beautiful cock. I'd forgotten, but suddenly it rushes back how perfectly we'd always fit together and how full he always made me feel—happy and satisfied and loved.

I haven't felt like that in a long time.

I reach for him, wrapping my hand around his erection. It's hot, smooth, and I make a few experimental strokes, while he groans and shuffles closer.

"Fuck, that feels good."

He gets on the bed with me and claims my mouth in a kiss. I keep stroking him, reacquainting myself with his heft, satisfied at the hiss he lets out when I press underneath the head, a favorite spot of mine to tease. "You're going to have to stop if you don't want this to end much too soon."

I still my hand instantly. I'm sure we could figure something out, but I'm greedy to feel him inside me.

He crowds against me on the bed, his naked body to my clothed one, grinds his cock into my thigh as he kisses me deep and hard.

Kissing. That was always another of my favorite things with Reed—the way he kisses makes me feel like the world could be burning around us and he wouldn't stop. The universe narrows down to our lips and breath and the heat we're generating between us. I'm definitely no longer cold. But my clothes are driving me crazy, especially this ridiculously tight pencil skirt.

I push him far enough away to finally take the damn thing off, losing my blouse, too, until I'm down to my black bra and underwear, nothing special, but not frumpy, since I believe underwear is a foundation you should feel good about, even on a random Tuesday.

My newly exposed skin is an invitation for Reed to move those world-narrowing kisses down my entire body. By the time he's mouthing over my left hipbone, my panties are soaked through and I'm desperate for some pressure on my clit. I reach down to touch myself, but he bats my hand away, replaces my fingers with his mouth. The electric pressure of his hot, wet mouth over the thin layer of cloth, rubbing and nipping against my clit, is too much. I shudder and cry out, coming for the first time at Reed's hands in six long years.

He takes off my underwear, rests two fingers at my entrance, as if to test my readiness. I borderline snarl at him. "Fucking get inside me already."

"Condom?" he asks.

"Fuck." I'm well-stocked, but it still takes way too long to get up and open my top dresser drawer, pull out two foil squares, and drop them on the bed. I unhook my bra while he's rolling on the lubricated condom. I leave on the pendant he gave me, the gold flashing and winking up at me from just above my breasts.

I used to hate that my tits were so small, but Reed said something to me once that made me see them in a different way. "Your body is perfect and if your breasts were bigger, you'd still be perfect, but I wouldn't be able to fit one entirely in my mouth at a time, and that would be a real shame." I laughed and rolled my eyes at him like I did whenever he got sappy about me, which was kind of a lot, but he was right. I liked that he could put my whole breast in his mouth, suck on it, pulling my small brown nipples to sharp, sensitive peaks. He used to do it for ages, just as focused on those as on kissing my mouth.

I don't care what you say about modern attention spans: in bed Reed is never in a hurry. He can spend forever on a single body part. Sometimes I found it annoying, wanting to hurry up and come. But more often, I'd be dizzy with pleasure and when I would finally orgasm, it would feel like it would take eons for the feeling to spiral through me. Later, I learned the term edging, and I wonder if that's what we were doing, unintentionally.

Mental note to ask Reed about that later. Right now, he's all wrapped and ready to go, but he's got one of my tits in his mouth and he's kneading the nipple of the other with his blunt fingers. I'm wriggling around, the sensations truly overwhelming.

"Please, can you...I know you want to be inside me."

"You're too delicious."

"Reed, seriously, please, I'm so wet."

He drags himself away from my breasts, which feel tingly, the skin around them scraped up from his scruff. "Yeah." He gives me one more kiss, then positions himself between my legs.

"What are you waiting for?" I ask, impatient. "It's not like it's our first time." I blame my overwhelming horniness for the casual way I throw that out there.

Reed, true to form, instead of sliding in and fucking the daylights out of me, stops and sits back on his knees, his erection jutting out in front of him like a tease. "It's not our first time. And this is not a one-time ex-sex thing for me. If it is for you, then maybe we should stop right now."

I stare at him in disbelief. "Seriously?" I know he's not trying to use sex as a weapon, trying to get me to agree to something because I want to come, preferably five minutes ago, but still. Timing.

"Seriously. Lani, I'm not saying we have to decide anything right now, but this is not one and done for me, and you need to know that."

It's not like when I kissed him in the kitchen I was thinking very far ahead. But I know what he means. We're not at the end of something here, we're at the beginning. It scares the shit out of me, but the idea of him walking out of here tonight and never seeing him again makes me want to barf. So I guess that means we're in this together.

"It's not one and done for me, either," I say. "I don't know what's going to happen. I can't guarantee I'm not going to make mistakes. But I want to see what happens with us."

"Us. Yeah. You and me. There's going to be an us, again." And he smiles, sweet and hopeful, and it pierces my heart and lets out some of the pain I've been walking around with since he left.

He's been hard this entire time, rather impressively so. I sit up on my elbows, gesture for him to come closer. He seals our agreement with a kiss, and then he's inside me, thick and full and perfect. It's different, again, from every other time I've had sex in my entire life. Because we're not exactly friends, we're not boyfriend and girlfriend, we're not even really husband and wife. But we're not just hooking up. We're all of that, we're none of it, we're something new, a combination of Reed and Lani that has never existed before.

His mouth barely leaves mine the entire time he's pumping into me. He's all I can taste, all I can smell, all I can feel, and it's so good to allow myself to be consumed, to allow myself to trust, to allow myself to be with someone who knows me better than maybe anyone else.

He snakes his hand down, thumbs my clit, and my body erupts for the second time tonight. He tears his mouth from mine, chanting my name, and comes deep and long. I pet his hair, damp with sweat, and push it off his forehead, kissing him lightly on the mouth as he rolls us to our sides in the nest of sheets.

"Us," I whisper.

From down the hallway, a loud buzzer goes off, startling me until I realize what it is.

"What the fuck was that?" Reed asks, pulling out of me, looking around wildly.

I giggle. "The washing machine. Your laundry is done."

"Christ. Give me a minute and I'll put it in the dryer."

"There's no rush," I say, snuggling against his chest. He isn't as soft as he used to be, but he still makes a great pillow, and I listen to the comforting thud of his heartbeat under my ear.

He's substantial beneath me, breathing and present. He might live on the other side of the country, I might have roots too deep to pull up here, maybe we have a lot of shit to work out. But I can't care about any of that when he's here, in the flesh, literally, the necklace he gave me pressed between us, the wedding ring we picked out together in the same drawer where I got the condom he just fucked me with.

We have a lot tangled up in each other, good and bad, and

we're choosing the harder path of trying to move forward together, tangles and all. I don't know if it's possible. I don't know if all we're doing is setting ourselves up to damage each other again. But I know anything else would feel like giving up. And I don't want to give up on this. Not again.

CHAPTER 24
REED

The clothes get dried. Dinner gets made. We take a shower and eat in our pajamas on the couch watching *Groundhog Day* for the five millionth time. It's pretty much the happiest I've ever been in my life.

We go back to bed and make love again, slower than the first time but no less intense. Lani is open with me, so free, and I'm goofy and effusive. She pretends not to like it, but I know she does.

We fit together, hand in glove. Years have passed but she tastes the same.

But the sex was never this good. I'll chalk it up to experience and move on. If I have anything to say about it, we'll be it for each other from now on.

That night, sleeping next to her in her bed, I dream about driving Lani's car. She's tucked against my side, which doesn't make sense because the 2002 doesn't have bench seats, but, hey, it's a dream. We're driving through the desert at sunrise, the sky is dark except for a sliver of orange at the horizon. I feel content because I have everything I need right there with me, but then I become confused. We're driving east, but the sky never gets lighter. We're still in darkness, and no matter how far I push the gas pedal down, no matter how fast the car goes, the sun never rises.

And then I wake up.

I shake off the feeling from the dream, because I have Lani tucked up beside me in real life, her thin arms and legs folded into herself, her ass tucked against my hips. It's the best way I've woken up in years. Two days ago, I woke up in this same bed, but she'd already gotten up by the time I opened my eyes. This is much better.

I'd stay like this forever, but we both have things to do today.

Lani's alarm goes off, irritatingly insistent, and she gropes her way toward turning it off. I stretch and admire the view of her ass clothed in nothing but a pair of tiny girly boxer shorts. She looks over her shoulder at me, effortlessly sexy. "Morning."

"Morning." I sit up and crack my neck audibly. "Sorry."

"It's okay."

We look at each other, each sorting through the proverbial morning after.

"I wish I didn't have to leave today."

"It's cool that you have more stops on your book tour, though."

"It's kind of surreal."

"I've got a busy day, anyway."

"You always do." I smile to show her I think that's awesome.

"True. Well. I'm going to get dressed. You want to use the bathroom first?"

"Sure." When I come out, she's fastening high-waisted dark blue linen pants, and wearing nothing but the pendant on her top half. My blood swiftly reallocates itself.

"Damn."

"What?"

"You're really hot."

She laughs and shakes her head. "Go make us coffee."

"Yes, dear." I detour by her on my way out of the bedroom so I can drop a kiss to her bare shoulder. I imagine I can hear her smile behind me.

The coffee maker is fairly intuitive, so I manage that, then I hunt around for a pan. The fridge is a jungle of green things. I find eggs and some spinach, and a block of Parmesan. By the time Lani comes out, fully dressed, sadly, with her face lightly made-up and gold hoops at her ears that go with the necklace I gave her, I'm scooping the spinach egg scramble onto two plates.

"What's this?" she asks, eyes wide.

"I made breakfast. Hope you don't mind."

"I don't mind. I'm a little bit in shock, but I don't mind."

"I'm a grown-up now. Grown-ups know how to make eggs."

"No, totally." She takes a bite even before she doctors her coffee. "Oh my God, these are really good, Reed."

"You'll have to teach me how to poach them. I've never done that before."

"Okay," she says. I permit myself a moment to enjoy her enjoying her eggs, then dig in myself.

"So what's on your agenda today?"

"Well, we have a lot of holiday orders already, so I'll be making sure our stock matches the orders. And I have an interview with a new PR firm we're thinking about hiring later. On the house-buying front, Beverly said we might set a closing date, which would be super exciting."

"I can't believe you're going to be a homeowner. That's so phenomenal."

"I have to stop myself from driving by to look at it literally every day. I don't want the neighbors to think I'm stalking someone and call the cops."

"Your car is very distinctive."

"But I could be moving in, like, thirty days, maybe. We'll see. Fingers crossed." She's compulsively tapping her nails against the side of her coffee mug. It's weird to see her so not chill about something.

"I'll help you pack," I say, looking around her place. She's going to need a lot of boxes for books.

"Will you?" She looks surprised. "Will you be coming back here that soon? I guess we haven't really talked about it."

"Do you want to talk about it?"

"I do. But not right now. I have to get to work."

"And I have to drive to L.A. But I could call you tonight? My second reading should be over by seven."

"Sounds good."

She gives me a lingering kiss by the doorway that has me really wanting to bail on all of my commitments and take her back to bed. As if she can read my mind, she scolds me. "Go! Do your author thing. We'll talk tonight."

I wonder if I'll ever feel okay about saying goodbye to her. It's only for a few days, but it feels wrong.

"Tonight," I murmur. I watch her walk out the door and memorize her soft, hopeful smile to keep me company until I can be with her again.

CHAPTER 25

LANI

"What's with you today?" Nicole asks suspiciously. She pushes back from her desk and crosses her arms. I know she won't let me deflect but I try anyway.

"What are you talking about? I'm being completely normal."

"You were humming. I think it was Taylor Swift."

"I was not! Don't be ridiculous." I try to school my mouth into my normal all-business face, but it's hard because the edges of my lips keep trying to curl up into a smile.

"No, seriously. And isn't that necklace from the Janice Sunshine collection?"

I consider telling her I bought it for myself, but remember I'm trying to be more honest with my friends, especially when it comes to Reed. "Reed bought it for me as a present."

"Oh, he did?" Her look of suspicion transforms into one of speculation. "So Reed is giving you jewelry and you can't stop humming and smiling. Did you get laid, Lani Kalama?"

"Look, I get laid all the time and I don't come into the office all smiley and shit."

"I know, that's why this is so incredible. Now I know what

you look like after you have sex with someone you actually have feelings for."

"Ugh. Please." But I'm aware I'm grinning and therefore have zero legs to stand on. "He spent the night," I admit.

"You have to give me more than that," Nicole begs. "Are you guys together? Are you going to do long-distance? Was it a one-time thing?"

"JFC, you are nosy, woman," I complain. "Just because you're married now and have to have sex with the same person for the rest of your life."

"That has nothing to do with anything." Nicole pouts. "Please. One detail?"

I sigh and give in. "Neither of us wants it to be a one-time thing, but it's complicated. We're going to try to do things differently than before, whatever that means. He had to go to L.A. for some book signings, but I think I'll see him again before he has to go back to New York."

"Oh, this is so exciting!" Nicole literally rubs her hands together. "I just realized you and Reed are going to be the only married ones in the group, besides me and Ricky."

That slows me down a little. I don't feel married. I feel like I'm at the beginning of a very new, very unexpected, very pitfall-ridden love affair. I have no idea what's going to happen next but settling into married life with Reed isn't exactly on my to-do list. I have so many other major things happening right now. Reed wasn't even on the list until a few days ago.

"I'm not looking for a big change. He knows my work is really important to me, he knows I'm buying a house, putting down roots in Santa Barbara. I've been really clear with him about all of that. Let's all of us take it one step at a time. And by 'us,' I mean you, Nicole Winesap."

"Do you think it's weird I didn't change my name? Nicole Kendell would sound good, too, right? Or Nicole Winesap-Kendell?"

Since we've debated this about a dozen times, I feel free to roll my eyes. "You don't need to change your name. Your identity isn't contingent on what is on your driver's license. Besides, I didn't change mine when I got married." I smirk at her.

"Boom! Lani with the marriage jokes. Though Lani Bennet sounds pretty good. Or how about Reed Kalama? Bennet-Kalama? No, definitely Kalama-Bennet."

"Stop!" I laugh and remember why I love my job so much. Because Nicole makes everything fun, even when she is driving me absolutely nuts.

"Speaking of, we should talk about your contract for these shell designs."

"Huh?" How is anything we were just talking about related to the drawings Reed steamrolled me into showing her?

"Your contract. I was going to propose the standard licensing agreement we offer to first-time designers, but I'm open to negotiating."

"You want to pay me for those designs? I assumed you'd incorporate them into the line."

"Dude, as part owner and manager of Winesap Design, your contract doesn't cover this type of thing. You need a contract."

I do some mental math. The fee for licensing the design plus any potential royalties is barely a fraction of my usual salary, but it's fair renumeration for the few afternoons I spent working on them. Weird to think in a few months I'll be able to point to a pillow or a shower curtain and tell people I designed the image that's on it. "Deal."

"I'll forward you the contract. Please return it by the end of the business day tomorrow," Nicole says primly.

"Return it to myself, you mean. Is that a conflict of interest?"

"I think we can cope. And seriously, if you ever have any other ideas you want to work up and run by me, do it. I love your style. I can't believe I didn't even know you draw."

"Reed and I used to do it a lot together. He's always been very encouraging of my creative side."

"He seems like a really good guy," Nicole says.

"He is, without a doubt, if nothing else, a good guy."

"So why didn't it work out?"

I grimace. "I told you. We were young. He wanted something really badly and he didn't realize I wasn't going to upend my life to be with him while he pursued his dreams. And I didn't realize our relationship was fragile enough that he could walk away." I frown. That's how I saw it, anyway. "I think. We haven't really talked about it."

"Hmmm. Well, I hope it works out, because it's really lovely to see you so happy, Lani."

"Thanks." I'm scared we're going to make the same mistakes all over again, but I'm more scared not to try to see this thing through, because I know there is no one else I'd want to try with besides Reed. It's super fucking cheesy and I will deny this if quoted, but he completes me.

I hope I complete him, too.

CHAPTER 26
REED

The motel I'm staying at in Pasadena isn't as nice as my place in Santa Barbara and is missing the most important thing: Lani.

But it's near to my second bookstore appearance of the day, so it's still fairly early by the time I drag myself into the room, along with my suitcase and a greasy paper bag that reeks of fries and onions.

My phone rings and I leap to answer it. "Hey," I say, breathless and excited to speak to Lani. I want to hear about her day and tell her about mine and in general be disgustingly couple-y.

"Hey yourself." Kingston's voice is disappointingly masculine and way too amused. "Either you thought I was someone else or your trip is going weirder than I expected."

"Fuck you. I thought you were Lani."

"Lani, your ex, Lani?"

"I'm pretty sure she's my ex-ex now. And we're supposed to talk tonight so I have to go."

"Hold up, please." I can imagine Kingston literally holding up his hand. He reminds me of Nicole, slightly, if Nicole were a gay, Black book agent with a penchant for paisley and fedoras. "I'm going to need particulars."

"Later, man, I'm starving, and she's expecting me to call."

"You sound both more assertive and more whipped than I've ever heard you, Reed Bennet."

"I live to keep you on your toes."

"Fine. Go have your phone sex with your ex-ex. I was calling to remind you about the schedule for tomorrow and to tell you Koko really wants to see pages next week at the latest."

Shit. The deadline. I'm supposed to have a mock-up of a thirty-two-page spread of the next Reed and Lucy book to my editor next week. I have more of the story now than when I flew here, but it needs a lot more work. I consider telling Kingston to ask for an extension, but even though the publisher would likely agree, I would be making the lives of a lot of people more difficult. The book is supposed to be the centerpiece of their spring catalog, which means meeting hard dates. I choke down the stress: I'll have to work over the weekend. I'd mentally set aside that time to relearn Lani's body intimately, before flying back to New York for the rest of the book tour, but she'll understand. Right?

This balancing act is going to be harder than I thought.

"Reed, man, you really need to stop zoning out when we're on the phone."

"Then why don't you text like everyone else?"

"I like the personal touch."

"I'll have the pages for Koko. I'll try to send them to you first, if you want."

"I want."

"Hey, man, I know I owe you already for getting those books sent to Ophelia's school—thank you, by the way, she was really stoked."

"Why does it feel like you're about to ask me for a big favor?"

"I'm...look, you were right, it has been a weird week. A life-changing one. If I didn't have those readings, I wouldn't come back to New York at all."

"Whoa. I knew you were ready to make a change, but this sounds drastic."

"I feel drastic. I'm ready to level up, man. I need to get my shit together, and I've given New York enough of my life. But I'm finally breaking up with the city. It's over. Which is why I was hoping you could work on closing the contract for the new set of Reed and Lucy books sooner rather than later."

Kingston whistles. "Makes sense. You can't woo your ladylove without dollar bills."

"It's not about that." It's a little bit about that.

"If you say so. I'll try, but there probably won't be any movement before next week."

"Fine. Thanks." I'm revved up on needing to make this change before I lose my nerve, but there's another thing I want to make clear. "You know you're what I'm going to miss most about New York, right?"

"Oh go on, now," he scoffs. "I'll still be your agent. Unless you're planning on firing me in this life reboot you're doing."

"Hell no," I declare. "You're stuck with me. And Reed and Lucy, until I run out of ideas or the public gets sick of them, whichever comes first."

"Sounds good. Hey, you be careful, okay? This girl broke you pretty hard once upon a time. You sure you know what you're doing?"

"I don't know. I only know we're trying to do things differently this time."

"Famous last words," he says darkly.

"Whatever, man. I gotta go. But thanks."

After hanging up, I have to eat or I'm going to pass out. The calorie infusion gives me a second wind, though I wish I had a beer to go with the burger and fries. A watered-down soda isn't doing the trick. Come to think of it, everything about this meal is subpar. If I were at Lani's there'd be wine. And vegetables. And her.

I hit her number on my phone. It rings so long I think it might go to voicemail, but she picks up at the last second.

"Hey," she says, out of breath like she was running for the phone.

"Is this a bad time?"

"I just got out of the shower. There was a glitter incident in the workshop today."

"Exploding unicorn?"

She laughs sharply, surprised. "No, thank God. That would probably have been even messier than what actually happened."

"You're naked right now? Sweet."

"You're such a romantic," Lani says. Her sarcasm means she likes me.

"I'm wearing the clothes you saw me in this morning, but I could get naked if that would even the score."

"Um, I'll think about it."

"Do that. So how was work, besides the glitter incident?"

"It was good. Busy. The holiday season feels like it starts earlier every year, but we're on track for thirty percent growth over last year, so I can't complain about that."

"You're remarkable. Any word on the house?"

"Yes, I almost forgot. We have a closing date! Right before Halloween. I have the inspection scheduled for next week. Things are moving fast now."

"That's fantastic."

"How did your book things go?"

"Not bad. The first crowd was a little small—you never know how many people are really going to show up. The second one was good, but it started at a weird time and I had to wait to eat until after and then I binged on too many fries. Feeling a little bloated, to be honest."

"When are you not? Honest, not bloated."

"I try to always be honest with you."

"Me too."

"Well, in the interest of honesty, I really miss you. I'd drive back and forth just to be able to sleep in the same bed as you."

"You would?"

"Do you want me to?" I eye the car key on the dresser and calculate how soon I could get there.

"No, that's dumb. I mean, it's a sweet idea, but you should stay put, get a good night's sleep. That's the kind of thing we'd do in college when we could operate on four hours of sleep and a Red Bull."

"Hey, speak for yourself. I can still pull an all-nighter if I have to. And I might have to. I have this deadline for the new book and I'm probably going to have to work this weekend."

"Okay."

"Right now, I want to hear more about how naked you are."

I feel her throaty laugh in my chest. "Actually, I put on some pajamas."

"Wow, you're good at multitasking. Can you talk on the phone and touch yourself at the same time, too?"

"Phone sex—are you serious?" She sounds half-incredulous, half-turned on.

"Oh, I'm serious." I let my voice drop to what I hope is a seductive register. "I'll bet it would be so easy to slip your hand into those tiny little pajama shorts you're wearing. They're basically underwear."

There's a pause, and Lani's voice comes back on, breathless and low. "Yeah. Why don't you join me."

It's not a request but an order I'm happy to obey. I make haste to unbuckle my belt and unbutton my fly. My cock's been half-hard since I first heard her voice, and now it only takes a few rough strokes to make me completely stiff.

I tuck the phone under my ear, and, thankful for my long arms, reach for the complimentary bottle of hand lotion on the in-room vanity counter without moving from my spot on the edge of the bed. The scent of almonds fills the air as I flip open the cap and squirt most of the bottle into my hand. I lube myself up and wish it was Lani touching me.

"Remember the time we got tipsy on White Russians at that *The Big Lebowski screening* and got each other off in the back row of the theater?" she asks.

I pause mid-stroke to recall that night, hazy in my memory. I have the impression of laughing and kissing and being young and reckless enough to finger Lani to completion right there in the movie theater. "I remember how wet you were under your skirt. How I sank my fingers into you. You were being too loud, so I had to kiss you to keep you quiet."

"I remember. I like it when you kiss me when you're inside of me." Her voice is low, a little breathy, and I imagine her hand working over her clit.

"Wish I was there right now, I bet you're dripping wet."

"Fuck." She sounds squirmy and desperate, a little like I feel. "I'm soaking."

"Yeah, you got your fingers up inside your pussy right now? God, I remember how it feels to have three fingers deep inside you, thumb on your clit. You feel so good, taste so good."

"Jesus, Reed." She sounds worked up, and I know she's imagining it, maybe doing it to herself. My own cock lets out a blurt of fluid at the image of her lying back on her bed, hand inside her shorts, working her own fingers into her wetness. I think about how slick and hot she must be. I can practically smell her dripping sex in this stark hotel room and I moan, feeling my orgasm steal up on me, too fast, too soon. I squeeze the base of my cock to draw it out a little longer.

"Can you come like that, baby?" The endearment slips out. "You ready to come?"

"I, I…keep talking," she orders, sweetly wrecked.

"That's it, baby, feel that perfect pussy. You're always so tight and hot. I wish I was there so bad to show you, to fill you up."

"Yeah. Yes. Reed." I can tell she's coming because she lets out a telltale noise, one that comes from somewhere deep inside her. "Fill me up," she says, "come on, do it, Reed."

My hand flies over my dick and I imagine being buried in her deep, not stopping until I'm coming. Rope after rope of come pulses into my hand, but with my eyes closed I imagine filling her up with it, just like she told me to. Fuck, that's hot. I take a few breaths to come down from the high. It wasn't as good as actually being with her, but it's a close second.

"Lani, fuck."

"Yeah, not bad," Lani says, a smile in her voice. "Not quite the discussion I thought we'd be having, but I don't mind."

"Me either." I wipe my hand with some tissues that have the texture of sandpaper and tuck myself away. "What did we have to talk about again?"

She laughs. "I honestly have no idea. Everything?"

"That sounds right." I yawn, the combination of greasy food and an orgasm pushing me to the edge of consciousness. "Did you know that *Reed and Lucy Go to the Movies* is the most-preordered book my publisher has ever had? I found that out today."

"Wow, Reed, you should be proud."

"I want you to know I'm really grateful for you. There would be no Reed and Lucy without you."

"You'd probably have come up with some other dazzling idea," she says. "But thank you."

I yawn again, trying to shield the noise from the phone but apparently unsuccessfully because Lani laughs again. "You get to bed. We can talk later."

"You sure?"

"I'm sure."

I let my tone drop an octave. "Sleep well." There's something else I want to say, but I can't say it for the first time in six years over the phone.

"You too," she says. Neither of us hangs up. It's classic high-school uncomfortable, not knowing how to sign off.

"Thanks for before," I say.

"Before?"

"You know, the smoking hot phone sex. If I'd known that was an option back in the day, maybe I would have tried to do long-distance."

The beat of silence before Lani says anything makes it perfectly clear that my poor attempt at humor was not well-received. "What?" she asks stiffly.

"No, sorry, bad joke. You're hot, I'm an idiot."

"Well. Goodnight."

Every instinct I have tells me I have to fix this, but for the life of me I don't know how. "Goodnight. I'll call you tomorrow."

"Okay."

She hangs up the phone.

CHAPTER 27

Hey, in between gigs, wanted to say hi.

Sorry, was in a meeting. Hi.

Just got out of another reading. If I never sign my name again, it'll be too soon.

Gotta take care of a supplier emergency in Goleta. Won't be able to talk today.

No worries. Good luck with your emergency.

* * *

Lani's birthday dinner is all set. Friday night, 5:45 p.m. at Mercy SB. You can Google the address.

And it's a surprise party, so don't tell Lani.

You can be trusted, right, Reed?

REED

I'm a vault

Good. You'll be there?

I will. Thanks for including me.

Well, from what I gather from Nicole you & Lani are two-for-one at the moment.

Are we now? Interesting.

The gossip circuit is very fast among people Nicole is friends with. It's a self-preservation thing.

I get that

See you then

* * *

KINGSTON

This is me texting you instead of calling you out of deference to the changing communication preferences of our generation.

REED

Welcome to the 21st century two decades late.

I'm making progress with the new contract. Should have details by early next week.

Awesome, thanks

And I'll give you the number of my cousin's moving company if you want it.

Definitely

Is everything OK? This is why I don't text. I need to hear your voice to make sure you aren't losing it over there without me.

I haven't been able to connect with Lani in a while and I said something stupid the other night & now I'm low key freaking out

She's going to have to get used to you spouting nonsense if you guys are going to be together

That makes me feel so much better

When are you seeing her again?

Tomorrow night. Her friends are throwing her a surprise birthday dinner

Then you better get her an A+ birthday gift

You're right. Money solves everything. Why didn't I think of that?

That was me being sarcastic, since we're texting and everything

Thanks for the tip

CHAPTER 28

LANI

It's another Friday afternoon. It's hard to believe it was only a week ago that I ran into Reed at Wild Child and my life was spun around like a top.

"So what are we doing for your birthday?" Nicole looks at me from her desk while I sift through my emails to make sure I haven't missed anything that can't wait until next week.

"It's not until Monday."

"Yeah, so? What are we doing? Drinks? Dancing? Should we all play hooky and go to Disneyland?"

"You know I hate Disneyland."

"You *think* you hate Disneyland. You've never been there with me, and I'm the Disneyland expert. Believe me, I'll make you love it."

"Why does that sound like a threat?"

"Not a threat, just a promise. But seriously. Birthday?"

"It's not even a major birthday. Thirty-one? Not sexy."

"Last year you told me you didn't want to do a big blowout for your thirtieth and I let you get away with that, because at the time I was obsessed with the engagement party and also Rosie's love life, but both of those things are now sorted."

"I'm not really into celebrating my birthday."

Nicole widens her blue eyes. "Why's that?"

"I don't know," I lie. "I don't want to make a big deal of it this year, either."

"Fine." Nicole pouts. "Then at least say you'll come to dinner tonight at Mercy SB. Kate and Oliver are coming up from L.A. for the weekend."

"I'm not sure." I'm exhausted, and Reed and I haven't talked since our phone sex ended on an off-note the other night. I think he's coming back into town today, and I'm in the unusual position of having to check with a guy before making plans. I can't say I like it.

"You know what, let's do it. I've got to eat, right?" Plus, when we go to Mercy SB with Oliver we always get VIP treatment, which isn't too shabby. There are perks to your best friend being the baby mama of the restaurant's owner.

"That's the spirit! Meet you there at six. Why don't you go home and change?"

"Change?" I look down at my outfit, a navy blouse and khaki linen pants. It's kind of conservative, but at least it's not covered in glitter. "Why? I look okay for Mercy, right?"

"You are stunning, as always. But you look a little work-y. A little corporate. I don't know, maybe put on a dress."

I narrow my eyes. "What's going on?"

"Nothing. Never mind. You look fine!"

Fuck. There's something going on and I'm too strung out to figure out what it is. "Okay, I'll go all the way back home to change and come all the way back over here for dinner. But you owe me."

"Anything," Nicole swears. "Shoo. See you at six."

It doesn't take me long to get home, and it does feel good to get out of the shoes I've been running around in all day. I check my phone before jumping in the shower. No word from Reed, so I toss off a text.

Heading out to dinner with some of the girls.

I bite my lip, wondering if I should ask him if he's planning on staying the night at my place. As far as I know, he doesn't have anywhere else to stay. Dammit. This is what we were supposed to talk about—logistics, how we're going to navigate being on different coasts. I haven't been in a relationship that lasted more than forty-eight hours since I was with Reed the first time. I'm not prepared for any of this.

When I get out of the shower there's a text waiting for me.

REED

Have fun!

Wow. Am I being blown off? How do you tell from a two-word text? Or maybe I'm overreacting and he wants me to have fun and not worry about him. Is that a thing? The Reed I used to know and I were fairly codependent. I don't remember us doing a lot of things with friends one-on-one in those last couple of years.

This is ridiculous. Reed and I are going to have a calm, rational conversation about all of this as soon as I can pin him down. In the meantime, I'm an essentially single, nearly thirty-one-year-old woman going out to dinner with her friends. I got this.

My all-purpose little black dress, with a big bow on the back, will look good with the pendant I haven't taken off since Reed fastened it around my neck. I reach for it, then reconsider, sliding the hangers in my closet all the way to the side so I can get at the seldom-worn fancy dresses in the way back. I bypass the California poppy-orange confection I wore as Nicole's bridesmaid. Even if it wasn't basically couture, it would be too over-the-top for Mercy. But there is one dress hanging there I think I can get away with.

I spend ten minutes wrangling my zipper, during which I

nearly text Reed for the use of an extra set of hands, pride be damned. Honestly, what's the point of having a boyfriend at all if he's not there to help you zip up the back of your dress?

I survey the results in the mirror. I look sleek, encased in a black skintight minidress, the ruched bodice showcasing my meager cleavage, the back half entirely see-through mesh from neck to sacrum. It's more appropriate for a movie premiere, which was, in fact, the occasion I got it for in the first place. Ricky had invested in a climate change documentary and brought Nicole and me to the Hollywood premiere. That might have been the night I made out with a certain B-list actor, but I don't kiss and tell.

I throw on my nicest black pumps, paint my lips carmine, fluff my hair, and I'm good to go. If it's too much for Mercy, for Santa Barbara, for Nicole, they can suck it.

I roll up to the valet right on time. It pains me to hand Makani over to a stranger, but I take comfort in knowing Oliver will rectify any damage that might get inflicted on my baby.

Mercy's always busy, but tonight it is positively hopping. There's a big crowd at the bar, and nearly every table is full. The hostess leads me to a semi-private circular booth in the farthest corner from the kitchen where we've held court once or twice since the place opened. I can see that's where we are tonight—Nicole and Ricky, and Kate and Oliver, as advertised, but they're not alone. Ophelia and Jamie, and Rosie and Gus are there, too. All of my best friends in the world and the men lucky enough to be with them.

And Reed.

Everyone's a bit dressed up, though not as outrageously as I am. Even Reed has donned a new-looking black button-down to cover up his ubiquitous T-shirt. It suits him, rolled up to the middle of his muscular forearms.

It's weird to see him, big as life, in the natural habitat of me and my friends. He looks like he fits in, yet he is a breath of fresh air. Seeing him feels good, if that makes any sense. My skin grows warm, my spine relaxes, and my smile, confused as it may be, is real.

Everyone seems to be smiling at me expectantly, as if waiting for a lightbulb to go off over my head. Suddenly Nicole's machinations become clear and I feel like a dope. She couldn't have been more transparent if she tried, and I walked straight into it. "Oh shit. Is this for my birthday?"

"Surprise! Happy birthday!" Everyone takes turns hugging me.

"We never do anything big for your birthday and I wanted to," Nicole says into my ear, giving me a boa constrictor squeeze. "Don't be mad, please?"

"I'm not mad." I'm not, though I'm not sure how I feel. They don't know why I tend to gloss over my birthday, why it's not the cause for celebration they might think it is. But far be it from me to get in the way of a good party. "Thanks. This is... great. What are we waiting for? Let's break out the bubbly!"

"Ahead of you on that," Oliver says, gesturing grandly. At the signal, three servers pop three bottles of champagne, to much clapping and hollering. Ricky sticks two fingers in his mouth and whistles. The servers make sure everyone has a glass. Reed brings one to me and clinks his against mine once it's safely in my hand.

"Happy early birthday, Lani."

My heart convulses, confronted with the intensity of his platinum-eyed stare. "Thanks. Did Nicole rope you into this?"

"Ophelia, actually."

"Seriously?" I glance over to my friend, who raises her glass to me. "Devious."

"Your friends really care about you."

"I'm lucky."

"And what is this dress? Are you trying to give me a heart attack?"

"I didn't even know you'd be here," I remind him. "I just wanted to dress up."

"Well, you look sensational."

"Thanks." We haven't touched or kissed hello or anything, which might have been okay if we'd done it right away, but now it's too late and everyone is watching us. It takes me a minute to identify how I'm feeling as *shy*.

I'm never shy. I don't celebrate my birthday. And I don't bring dates to dinners where all my friends are paired off like lovebirds. This isn't me.

"I've taken the liberty of ordering for the table," Oliver says as he gets us to settle into our seats, Reed on my right, Oliver on my left so he can get up and have access to the room if necessary. A restaurateur's work is never done. "But it's your party, Lani, so anything you want, say the word."

"As long as burrata is involved, I'm golden," I say. "And Brussels sprouts for Kate." Everyone laughs—Kate's love of the restaurant's caramelized Brussels sprouts is well documented.

"I think she's eaten so many Brussels sprouts the baby's going to come out marinated in balsamic vinegar," Oliver says.

"Or smelling like cabbage," Kate offers.

After that, I'm able to pretend this is a regular dinner with friends, no special occasion. Reed slots into the group like he has been here all along, getting along sickeningly well with everyone. He talks books with Ophelia and Rosie, asks intelligent questions about the patent Jamie applied for for his new 3D printer design. Gus seems to have him primed to go surfing at the next available opportunity, even though as far as I know Reed has never so much as touched a surfboard before.

It's hard not to feel like the outsider once again, the one who doesn't really belong. Reed belongs, with his creative job, his manly bonhomie. I'm just the number cruncher who sleeps around. I'm not someone's girlfriend. I'm definitely not someone's wife.

I listen to everyone talk and laugh and we all eat, eat, and eat some more, as a parade of Mercy's sublime modern California-Moroccan dishes arrive.

"That's it," Reed says eventually, leaning back in his chair and folding his arms over his stomach. "I can't eat anything else. I'm dead."

"Death by Mercy's food is a good way to go," Gus says.

I'm a bit bloated myself. I've almost been able to forget this is a birthday party, but my friends won't let me. They bring out a cake, candles and everything. I stoically endure the off-key singing and glance over at Reed, his face glowing in the candlelight, then I blow out the candles and make my wish. He smiles at me, but I can't help thinking that the wish I'm silently forming will never come true.

Between bites of cake the girls pass me a series of beautifully wrapped boxes.

"What's this? Seriously, you don't need to do presents, too. You're spoiling me." I'm honestly not used to being the center of attention, content with being the snarky worker bee sidekick to Nicole's queen.

"Come on, you never let us spoil you." The queen herself pouts.

"What's your birthday for if not for other people to make a big deal out of it?" Jamie says.

"Open mine first." Rosie pushes a turquoise-wrapped box toward me. I open it, hating the feeling of everyone's eyes on me. Inside is a gift card to a bed and bath store. "For your new house!"

"And now mine," Kate says. "The pink one."

It's a gift card to my favorite kitchen store in Santa Barbara. "You guys." I sniff. I refuse to cry.

Ophelia's is a gift card for bed linens, and Nicole's is for furniture. They're all being way too generous and thoughtful, and I'm...

"Overwhelmed," I say. "I'm overwhelmed."

Reed puts his hand on my arm, the first time he's touched me all night. It helps a little.

"Thanks, everyone."

"To Lani," Reed says, raising his glass.

"To Lani," everyone echoes.

It's the straw that breaks this camel's back. I get up from the table abruptly as everyone's still toasting.

"I'll be right back." And I run.

CHAPTER 29

REED

I find Lani washing her hands in the trendy unisex washroom of Mercy SB, her face taut with tension.

"You okay?"

"I'm fine."

"You want to go home?"

She shakes her hands, presses one to the back of her neck. "No. I just need a second. Everyone's so wonderful. It's a little bit much."

"I know your birthday isn't your favorite thing."

She smiles wryly. "I guess my friends never got the memo."

"You never told them?"

"Told them what?"

"Why you don't like your birthday."

She's quiet. An older man comes through on his way to the men's room side. When we're alone again she says, "You know why?"

"You told me."

Lani is the most magnificent woman I've ever met, and right now, in her stunning skintight dress, her expressive face shutters. She looks small. The sight terrifies me. I take a step closer to her, but her body language tells me she doesn't want me to touch her.

"Then why did you do it?" she whispers.

"Do what?"

"Leave me. To go to Iowa. You knew he left us and it has never stopped hurting. And then you left me. Did you know what you were doing to me?"

There it is. The question for the ages. Why did I leave the woman I loved, who I had recently made my wife, to pursue my own dreams when I knew her own father had left her as a kid —*on her birthday*—and she'd never gotten over it?

Was I that much of an asshole?

"I can't defend myself, Lani. But since we didn't have this conversation at the time, you deserve to know I honestly thought with all the wisdom of a twenty-two-year-old that you'd come with me. I never thought I was leaving you. I didn't want to." It would never have occurred to me to blow up my relationship with Lani. Even then I knew she was the best thing that ever happened to me.

"I thought if I didn't go to Iowa my career would never happen. In my mind, if I did the program, I could make great things happen for us. I'd write a bestseller and I'd be able to support you and be the partner you deserved. In a twisted way I thought I was doing it for us."

Lani huffs, and I know how dumb it sounds in retrospect.

"But now I know I was doing it for me. Maybe I needed to do it, to learn that it wasn't the be-all and end-all I thought it was, but believe me, it didn't make me happy. I ached being apart from you.

"And I have so many regrets. That I didn't handle telling you better, that I didn't talk to you about our options. Once I was there and I realized what was happening, that we were breaking up, I should have stopped the world to get back to you. But I didn't. I'll always regret that. But I never stopped loving you. And these last few days, I know for sure. You are impossible for me not to love."

I reach out, wanting to fold her to me, to protect her from the pain I caused, six years too late, but she shrinks back.

"No. No. You don't get to decide this again. You made me love you. You made me think it made sense to marry you because I loved you so goddamned much. And then you left. It felt like my dad leaving me all over again. I know intellectually you—he—didn't leave because of something I did or didn't do, but I was still devastated."

She sucks in a shaky breath and my heart feels like it's being ground under the sole of her black high heel, but I earned that.

"I missed you so much. And to be fair, to my twenty-four-year-old self, it never occurred to me to follow you, even if I'd wanted to leave the life we were building here. I thought if you loved me, you'd stay, and when you didn't it meant you didn't love me. I convinced myself I was better off without you.

"Now you're here and you're saying it was a mistake, but it's too late. I'm a Never a Bride, maybe the only true one." Her posture goes rigid, as if she's just donned a suit of armor.

I don't buy it. "Really, Lani? Then why did you lie about me? Why didn't you serve me with papers years ago? Why didn't you call a lawyer the first day I showed up in town? If you want me out of your life so badly, why am I here tonight, to be counted among the people who love you? Because I do. I love you, Lani. And you can't tell me this doesn't feel right."

She shakes her head. "It doesn't. I'm not that person."

"Yes, you are. You were that person when we met, when you did me the enormous honor of being with me. That Lani still exists. She's more real than the one who thinks she has to do everything by herself—"

"Stop," Lani cries.

The man from before comes back to wash his hands, and Lani takes the opportunity to slip past me and head for the table.

My molars grind together in frustration. I know I fucked up then, I'm fucking up now, I'm probably not done fucking up, honestly. But I know that she's not giving herself enough credit. She deserves to let herself have more than an empty house, to watch her friends fall in love while denying love to herself.

I hustle back to the table in time to see Lani pick up her purse and the gift bag of her presents. She's leaving?

"I'm beat," she says to the group with a fake smile.

"Can I talk to you for a second?" I ask, touching her elbow.

"I think we're done talking." She pulls her arm away sharply. I feel eight pairs of eyes on us and resist the urge to look to them for help. I know I'm the odd man out here. I'm on my own. This is my fault and I have to fix it myself.

Then she picks up her things and walks out.

I watch her leave, torn about going after her. My every instinct to this point has apparently steered me wrong. Why should this time be any different?

The eight of them are scrutinizing me. I catch Ophelia's gaze first. Her eyes are wide. I can tell she's trying to stay neutral and losing. I'm not her friend. "You should probably give her space," she says, her voice hard.

"I'm sorry," I say, as if that'll do any good.

"You know, Lani's kind of touchy about her birthday," Nicole says. "And it's been a long week. She's probably tired. After a good night's sleep you two can work this out."

I appreciate her optimism, but I'm not sure that's what this is going to take.

"I have to go," I say, booking it out of there without looking back. There goes my dream of slotting into this pre-made life like a wooden doll plopping himself into a dollhouse already furnished with friends.

Lani's waiting for the valet to bring around her car, shoulders hunched over, arms wrapped protectively around her middle.

"Look, maybe you don't want to hear this right now, but I need you to know I want to be in your life again. I want to be with you."

She looks up tiredly. "Did you forget we live in different time zones?"

"I'm going to move here. I can't date my wife from across the country."

"Yes, we both know how incapable of long-distance relationships you are," she snaps.

Ouch. "I hurt you and I'm so, so sorry."

She lets out a stunned gasp. I freeze, realizing what's come out of my mouth. Have I ever apologized to her before? If I haven't, I'm an even bigger screwup than I thought.

"I'm sorry, Lani." I speak every word deliberately, hoping my sincerity shows through. I can't believe it's taken me so long to connect the dots on this. "I think I wrote Reed and Lucy to try to make amends for how badly I messed up. Clearly, I have a lot of work to do in that department, but please say you'll let me try."

Lani's car pulls up to the curb and idles reproachfully at us. I want so much for her to invite me in, to take me home, to let me show her how hard I'm going to work to be worthy of her.

She looks at the car, blows out a breath, and looks back at me.

"Reed, it doesn't matter how much you loved me or how stupid we both were. We did what we did and now we are who we are and you're right."

"About what?"

"We need to do what we were too afraid to do the first time."

"What do you mean?" There are a lot of things I want to do differently from the first time.

"A clean break."

I can't be hearing her right.

"We should get a divorce."

CHAPTER 30

LANI

I don't stick around the outside of the restaurant to see Reed's reaction to my dropping the d-word. For one thing, I'm freezing. I blast the heater the whole way home, but I can't seem to warm up. Once home, I stand under the spray of the shower, shivering, teeth chattering. I still can't get warm.

I dry off, put on my Christmas pajamas, red flannel ones, and wrap myself in three layers of blankets in my bed. It's only then, when I'm protected from the world by four layers of fabric and I have nowhere else to hide, that I start to cry.

* * *

Morning finds me blanket-less, my body's ability to regulate its temperature apparently restored in the night. The sun coming through my bedroom window is heating up the room and I'm stifling in my flannel. I strip off the seasonally inappropriate clothes and put on a casual housedress. Saturday often finds me at the farmers market, but I'm not sure if I'm up for being around other humans at the moment.

I make myself coffee and a green smoothie, then grab my sketchbook and get in Makani to head to my favorite beach,

Rincon Point. With the windows rolled down and the late September sunshine warming up the car, I don't need to listen to the radio to keep thoughts out of my head on the drive—the wind and the traffic noises are enough.

Once parked, I find the path to the beach, the scent of brine in my nose. I ditch my shoes at the base of the path and relish the way the sand pushes between my toes. I pick my way over the large rocks that form a natural break and find a place to settle. There are a few surfers, bobbing like buoys fifty yards out, but the best waves of the day have already passed. Even so, the morning hasn't advanced enough for the beach-going families to show up. I have this stretch of beach to myself.

I open my book to a fresh page. As a kid I used to sketch constantly. I liked to find interesting pieces of seaweed and pretty rocks and try to get them as lifelike as possible on the page. I'd tear out pictures of models from magazines and attempt to replicate their photo-reality with my pencil. I never cared much about photography, but it pleased me to be able to draw something that when looked at the right way could perhaps be mistaken for real life.

My dad always heaped praise on my drawings. He'd buy me sketchbook after sketchbook to fill up, even when my mom complained. Not that she didn't encourage my artistic side, but she was always the practical one, even before Dad left. She'd grown up poor, put herself through college, then nearly repeated the cycle by having my sister and me too young. She misses me, and she knows I'm never moving back to Hawaii, but she has always been incredibly supportive of my business aspirations.

When she found out my relationship with Reed was getting serious, she cautioned me to take it slow. She didn't want me to make the same mistakes she did, obviously. I never told her that Reed and I made one huge mistake: getting married. When he left and it became clear things were over between us, she was tactfully supportive, but I could tell she was relieved I wouldn't have the distraction as I finished up my MBA and started my career.

What would she say now if I told her I'd almost made the same mistake twice?

What would she say if I told her I regret every minute I spent apart from Reed?

She'd probably call me a fool.

I don't need her to tell me what I already know.

He and I both messed up back then, and we both messed up this time thinking things could be different. But I'm the same girl who doesn't want to be left behind. He's the same impetuous boy who acts before he thinks, who believes love is enough to fix everything.

He did say that last night, didn't he? I haven't gotten a declaration of love in a while, so maybe it went over my head, but I'm pretty sure he said he still loves me. Or loves me again. Or something.

"What am I doing?" The question's out there, but the foul-tempered seagull stalking my spot isn't providing any good answers.

Last night, accepting Reed's love seemed impossible and fixing our problems seemed insurmountable. I was also tired, emotionally overwhelmed from a surprise birthday party, and having a six-year-overdue breakup fight with Reed. Somewhere in there, I turned the breakup of the past into a breakup of the present.

But I don't feel any relief at having shut the door on us.

I thought it would make me feel better to let go of any hope of us being together. Instead, I just feel sad. I'll have to mourn him all over again. And this time it's me who pushed him away, instead of him taking us for granted.

I look down at my sketchbook. It's as blank as the rest of my future. Why am I buying that big house to knock around in alone? Why am I putting in extra hours at work only to come home to takeout and television? The idea of going back to my usual social life, picking up guys whenever I have the itch, holds no appeal. Every single one of my friends is paired off, the fucking traitors, and I'm going to be alone. Forever.

I pull out my phone, intending to put the members of the Never a Bride group chat on blast. Nicole, I can't fault for being a hypocrite, sadly, but I can make her feel bad about throwing me a birthday party I told her I didn't want.

I had turned my phone off last night before I got into the shower. It chimes on, and I'm barraged with a series of texts.

The first ones are from last night.

NICOLE

Everything OK?

I'm assuming you're with Reed, since he left right after you.

Call me tomorrow, k?

OPHELIA

Just checking on you, Lani. Hope we didn't go too overboard with the birthday thing.

KATE

Oliver wants to know if you have food poisoning. If so, he will fire someone. He might be kidding.

ROSIE

If you have food poisoning, try to stay hydrated. It will likely pass within 24 hours.

OPHELIA

Why would she have food poisoning? We all ate the same things.

KATE

Oh right. I don't know. Where is she then?

ROSIE

Maybe she and Reed need some alone time.

OPHELIA

Well, let me know if you want to meet up at the
farmers market tomorrow.

KATE

Good night, ladies.

ROSIE

Good night. Thank Oliver again for us.

There's one from my mom from this morning.

KAIA KALAMA

Hey sweetie. Can we talk about your next
visit? Thanksgiving? Christmas? I know the
tickets are 💰 but I want to see you. Call me.

And finally, one from Reed, from late last night.

REED

You were right about everything. I'm sorry.

I stare at the message until the screen goes black.

CHAPTER 31

REED

REED

> She wnts divorce. I want whiskey. Do u have whiskey?

KINGSTON

> Are you seriously drunk texting me at 8 a.m. my time?

My time is your time

> You're back?

> Never mind. I was sleeping.

> Alone, more's the pity.

Srry. I can't do anything rite

> You in your apartment?

I thinkso

Drank it all

> Stop drinking. Unless it's water.

Lani ended things

I'm sorry, man, hang in there. You can get
through this.

Reed?

I'm assuming you passed out and have not
choked on your own vomit.

The buzzing in my ear is distinct from the ringing in my head but no less annoying. I crack open my eyes and instantly wish I hadn't. I have a splitting headache, and my mouth is as dry as if I'd eaten one of those silica gel do-not-eat packs.

The buzzing is coming from the phone but it's not a text.

I manage to answer the call and croak into the phone. "What?"

Kingston gets right to the point. "Let me in."

I stagger to my feet, fighting through a wave of dizziness and make it to the intercom box on the wall by my apartment door. I hit the button on the second attempt, then look around blearily trying to recall the chain of events that led me to pass out fully dressed on my living room floor. Another glance at my phone shows it's nearly noon. My roommates are nowhere to be seen. Either they're not around, or they managed to get up and step around my prone body without waking me. Not sure if I'm touched at their thoughtfulness or reinforced in my belief that they couldn't care less if I live or die.

It takes my sluggish brain the entirety of Kingston's journey from the street to my third-floor door to parse the various levels of my misery. I'm hungover, that much is clear. Malt liquor on top of airplane cocktails was not my smartest impulse, but the real reason for my anguish is a lithe five-foot-seven bundle of hope and despair. I've never been able to do right by her. Not then. Not now. And she's cutting me off. So not ever, I guess.

The excruciating minutes after Lani drove away from me at the restaurant filter back. I was paralyzed by my need to go after her and completely certain she didn't want me to, so I didn't. Instead, I retrieved my suitcase from Mercy SB while avoiding the questioning glances of Lani's friends. The driver of the ride I ordered to take me to the airport agreed to make a stop at Winesap Design, where I slid an envelope under the front door. I made it to LAX in time to take a redeye to New York. I vaguely remember drinking cocktails on the flight, and then the slog from JFK in the early morning hours, with a stop at a convenience store for two forties of Colt 45.

A knock on the door activates the pounding in my head.

"Open up, Reed."

I fumble open the door and Kingston is there, dapper in a pea coat and scarf, and carrying two paper cups that I hope to Christ contain coffee.

"Am I hallucinating you?"

"I'm real, baby," he says, letting himself into the room. "I wish I were hallucinating you. You are a vision in wretchedness."

"I don't feel good," I say, sitting down heavily on the ratty couch. "I might still be drunk."

"No shit."

"Lani wants a divorce."

"So you said."

"When did I say that?"

"You texted me last night, and I surmised it would be in both of our best interests if I came to do damage control. Voilà, your fairy godfather." He gestures to himself extravagantly.

"I think I'm going to throw up."

"Have at it," he says, quickly moving out of the way.

Twenty minutes later, I've emptied out, showered, and put on my most comfortable pair of jeans and my Eric Carle Museum shirt.

"Here." Kingston hands me a bottle of water, which I sip gingerly. "You up for coffee? I can warm it up."

"Kill me now."

"No can do. You have a deadline. I can't kill you until after you make that."

I think over the maybe eighty percent-done book and groan. "Oh God. You're going to have to ask for an extension."

"We'll see."

"And Kingston, I think I need to stop writing Reed and Lucy. I know I said I wanted that contract, but I can't do it anymore. I'll finish this one and then it's over."

"Yep, just as I thought. Let's go."

"Where?"

"To the diner around the corner. Its Yelp rating isn't great, but it can't be worse than the place we went to by the airport that one time."

"The place with the moldy bagels?" I clutch my stomach, considering my need to vomit again.

"You okay?"

I take another sip of water. "TBD."

I bless the inventor of sunglasses as we walk the two blocks to the diner. It's one of those sunny, beautiful New York days that feels like the last day of summer before it starts getting cold. Coffee helps, even if it's mediocre, and after the ibuprofen Kingston made me swallow back at my place starts to kick in, anything greasy sounds amazing. We order and I sink my head down on my folded arms.

"You want to tell me exactly what happened? The last time we talked you were all about moving to California to be with your ladylove. I assumed she was copacetic. Now she wants a divorce? What did you do?"

I whimper. "It's complicated."

"I have time."

"I'm twenty-eight years old and I'm as clueless as I was when I was twenty-two and dumb as shit."

"How, specifically?"

"We were all having dinner for her birthday, only she hates her birthday. Her dad left her and her mom and her sister on her eighth birthday. She was holding up okay, but something made her freak out and we started fighting. She reminded me that back then I was well aware her dad left her, and then I went and did the same thing." I still feel sick thinking about how callous I must have seemed to her, how blind I was not to make the connection.

"I can never make up for that and I don't deserve to. She's right to kick me to the curb. What have I ever done for her? I gave her some money for her house because I felt guilty that I mined our relationship and our dynamic for the Reed and Lucy books. Meanwhile, she's flourished, and I thought I'd grown up, made something of my life, too, but I'm the same. I'm not even a real writer. I draw childish pictures and put some captions on them."

"Okay, that's where I stop this pity party." Kingston smiles at our server as they drop a small pig's worth of bacon on the table and refill our coffees. "You are a writer. You make a good living creating books that thousands of people have enjoyed and continue to enjoy. Yes, you used your life experience to write them, but that's what artists do. Reed and Lucy is bigger than Reed and Lani. So many people—adults and kids alike—would be disappointed if you stopped writing the series. Not to mention your bank balance. And good luck getting someone to pick up your next book. Do know how hard it is to launch a successful series in this saturated market?"

"So says the man who gets fifteen percent. Ow!" I rub my ear where Kingston cuffed me.

"Seriously, Reed. Self-sabotage might be your thing, but it is not a good look. If you sincerely need an extension to make the next Reed and Lucy book decent, I will call Koko first thing Monday and get you one. But please take a little time to think about the future of the series. I'm in negotiations right now. It's my reputation on the line, too."

"I'll think about it, but I don't know if I can do it. I fucked up with Lani and if this is... She said we needed a clean break. Not the fading away we did the first time. That means she won't be in my life at all, not even as a ghost. Only as a memory. I don't know how I'm going to be able to write like that."

"You will because you're a professional. Besides, I'm not convinced things are really over between you."

"What part of she wants a divorce isn't clear?"

"She had years to ask you for a divorce and she never did. This is just like Reed and Lucy. They fight, they make up. I've never met the woman, but I have a feeling about this. You and Lani are meant to be together. We just need to figure out what happens next in the book."

"What? Is this some meta thing? I'm too hung over for existentialism."

"Eat your bacon." Kingston pulls out his cell. "What's the name of her shop?"

"Winesap Design. Why?"

"Flowers."

"I'm sorry, what?"

"Flowers, step one in wooing back your wife before she can become your ex-wife."

"I don't think she's working today."

"Hmmm. Well, what is she doing today?"

"She usually goes to the farmers market, I think. Her friends might know. Except I'm pretty sure they hate me right now."

"Jesus, it sounds like this birthday dinner was really an epic fail."

"It was *The Odyssey* of fails."

"Come on, give me something to work with."

"She's buying a house. It's this classic Craftsman, but it

needs some work. She's closing in a few weeks. Is there something there?"

"Flowers. Friends. House. You on your knees, groveling. I think we have some decent pieces of the puzzle."

"Good. I'm going to go sleep for a year. Wake me up when you've solved my life."

"Not so fast. What about *Reed and Lucy Go to School*? Is it going to be ready?"

I think about all the work I put in on it yesterday when I was riding high on my plans and hopes, looking forward to surprising Lani and sharing my investment in our future. It's close, but I don't know if I have the heart to finish it now that it's been impaled on the heels of Lani's stilettos.

I look at Kingston. He sold my first book, got me my first multi-book deal. He sold foreign rights and a TV option and merchandise so I could give up temping and do the work I always dreamed about doing. Is it the same thing I thought I'd be doing when I went off to be the next great American novelist? No. But I'm a working author, a dream pursued by many, achieved by few. Once again, I'm being a goddamned baby. I am a professional, all recent evidence to the contrary.

"No extension. The book will be ready on time, I promise."

"Now you're talking." He crunches on a piece of bacon. "This isn't bad. Crispy. What are you going to do about Lani?"

"I don't know. I don't know if she wants me to do anything. She was pretty clear last night."

Kingston's face loses its "everything's going to be okay" smile. "Are you going to be all right if it's over between you for real?" he asks gently.

My stomach clenches and it's not the grease or the hangover. She is the only one I've ever wanted and the person who knows me the best in the whole world. But she's got the right to protect herself from someone who has messed things up perhaps beyond fixing.

"I'll have to be."

"And you're still moving to California?"

Will it be the same knowing I'll be starting over yet again, more alone than ever? No. But it's where I belong, and I have to trust I'll find some kind of life there, even if it's not perfect and ready-made. "Yeah. I'm for sure leaving. But after I get my shit together. I have a deadline."

CHAPTER 32

LANI

I send a couple of texts to assure the girls I'm alive and not about to throw myself into the Pacific. Then I call Mom.

"Keikilani, I'm so glad you called. I'm looking at the calendar. Thanksgiving is going to be here before you know it. Your sister's not coming home, and I figure you'll still be unpacking, so maybe you both can come back at Christmas? Unless you want to have Christmas in your new house? Maybe I should come there."

I haven't thought about the holidays at all, besides ramping up staffing for the store and ordering the holiday decorations.

"I was actually thinking maybe I should come sooner. Things have been wild and I really need a break."

"Is everything okay?" Mom's tone doesn't change. I know she cares about me and worries about me, but she's no-nonsense about most things. She's always had to put the practical ahead of the emotional in order to survive.

"Not really."

"Keikilani, you know you always get like this around your birthday. I sent your present to the store, by the way. Your favorite macadamia nuts. You are such a Hawaiian cliché sometimes."

"It's not because of my birthday."

"Then what?"

"Well, maybe a little."

"Tell me."

"Remember Reed Bennet?"

"Your ex-boyfriend who writes the picture books?"

"That's the one. He came to town to visit. We...well, there's a lot of unfinished business between us, apparently, and we were thinking about getting back together. But it—I don't know. It all blew up and I think I made a big mistake. I told him we needed a clean break. But I'm not sure that's what I really want."

"And you want to come hide out here? How will that fix anything?"

I kick the sand at my feet like a sulky child. "He ran away on me last time. I guess I wanted to run away on him for a change."

"Honey, has running ever helped anyone? Your father ran away, and he ended up dead."

"Jesus, Mom."

"You're thirty-one, you can handle it. Your dad left us, which honestly was for the best."

We don't talk about him very often. "How can you say that?"

"A bad dad is worse than no dad at all."

"I guess so. It's hard to believe that when you have nothing to compare it to."

"Lani, you've held on to the good memories of your father, and I really admire you for that. That car you've poured so much money into is pretty much a shrine to him."

"I love that car," I say stubbornly.

"I know you do, honey. And I know you loved your dad. And he loved you and your sister, in his own way. But he wasn't good for me, or us, and when he left it was a relief, honestly. I'm sorry he died the way he did, so suddenly. I know you always thought you might reconcile with him one day. But don't you want to let go of that?"

I let out a frustrated breath. "I thought I had. I guess I'm not as well-adjusted as I thought I was."

"I couldn't be prouder of you, Lani. You've educated yourself, you're terrific at your job, you've given me security, you're buying your first house. It's a beautiful house. But when you sent me the pictures, I couldn't help but think it's so much room for you. You wouldn't have chosen it if you hadn't wanted to share it with someone. Be honest. Is Reed someone you think you could share your life with?"

Dammit. Was Reed right? Have I been building my life on the lie that I'm not the kind of person who wants what Reed is offering me? Why can't I seem to let myself want what I want? Why can't I be okay with being me, even if that means I'm leaving myself vulnerable to being left again?

"I want to, makuahine," I whisper. "I want to so much."

"Then tell him that's what you want. Any man who is lucky enough to be chosen by you is going to be smart enough to fall to his knees and tell you he'll move heaven and earth to deserve that chance. Let him do that for you."

"You think that'll work?"

"If it doesn't, I'll eat my hat."

"You never wear a hat."

"I'll eat my imitation Prada sunglasses."

I laugh. "Okay, Mom. You won't mind if I end up with a white boy who wears leather bracelets unironically?"

"You can support him, right? He'll be handy around the house."

I highly doubt Reed knows anything about home maintenance. But he did learn how to cook eggs and do laundry, so there's hope.

"Sure. He can be my househusband."

"Husband? What happened to being Never a Bride?"

Shit. I forgot for a minute she's still in the dark about my marital status. Best save that reveal for another day. "Uh, I gotta go. Thanks for the pep talk. I'll keep you posted about Christmas."

"Love you, silly girl."

"Love you, too."

I hang up before I get into further trouble. But my mother is right. If I want Reed, I'm going to have to accept the wounds of the past and move on. I'm going to have to accept that my dad leaving has nothing to do with Reed and me. And I'm going to have to hope he's still willing to take me just as I am—workaholic, finicky about my space, obsessive about my car, loyal to a fault with my friends. But I'm willing to make space for him.

I take my time walking back to Makani. The drawing session was a bust, but I feel clearer about a few things. I love Reed. I don't know if I never stopped or if seeing him again has made me certain that I'm never going to feel this way about anyone else, but it doesn't matter. I messed up last night, and I need to fix it.

First stop, Winesap Design. Macadamia nuts will help me think, and my mom said she sent my birthday package to the shop.

I don't have my work keys, so I have to go in the front. It's fairly busy, with all three floor staff members helping customers. I let myself back through the cash wrap, nip through the stock room, and sift through the mail on my desk.

Score, a priority-mail box from Mom and what looks like a birthday card from my sister. That's sweet. Akela and I aren't super close, but there's no bad blood. She's just very into her career as a successful professional video game player while I can't be bothered to figure out Tetris, so our interactions are limited.

There's also a plain business-sized envelope with my name on it. I recognize Reed's spiky handwriting. Slowly, I set down the box and the card and pick up the envelope. It's light. I tear it open carefully. Inside is a check for twenty-five thousand dollars made out to me. Attached is a sticky note.

> *Lani,*
> *I'm sorry for everything. I want you to have this.*
> *Don't worry, I won't be taking up your guest room*
> *anytime soon. I'm so proud of you.*
> *Reed*

I stare at the little yellow square of paper until the words blur together.

I never thought the number of words someone could fit on a sticky note could gut me so thoroughly. But I know what this means. Reed is gone.

* * *

LANI

SOS

I need help

Meet me at the shop ASAP

NICOLE

OK

KATE

Coming

OPHELIA

15 min

ROSIE

On my way

* * *

"Macadamia nut?" I've been stress eating for twenty minutes and my jaw aches. I offer the jar to my assembled girlfriends.

"No thanks. What's the SOS? We've been worried about you since last night." Nicole is the unofficial spokeswoman, as everyone looks at me anxiously from their various perches in the back office of Winesap Design.

I sigh. "Here's the deal. I fucked up. I was upset last night, for lots of reasons, and Reed and I had a fight and I told him we should"—I can't help the reflexive shudder at my recklessness—"stop all this pretending we could be a real couple again and get a divorce."

The four of them collectively wince.

"But I've been doing a lot of thinking, and the thing is, I don't want that. I look at all of you, and how happy you are and how you've chosen different paths since I've known you, and I want to be able to choose a different path for myself if that's what I want. You all are so brave, and I want to be brave."

I risk a glance up. Ophelia's warm brown eyes are comically round, Kate's blue eyes squinty, like she's trying not to cry. Rosie is reaching into her purse for a tissue, and Nicole sweeps her dark blond lashes up and down rapidly.

"Shit. I cried enough last night, don't make me do it again," I complain.

"It's okay, Lani. We're here for you." Rosie sniffs. "What can we do to help?"

"I'm sure Reed would be overjoyed to have you tell him you want to try again," Nicole declares.

"I think he left to go back to New York already."

Kate cringes. "Too late for a sprint to the airport?"

"I texted him and he didn't text me back. So either he's in the air or he doesn't want to talk to me. Either way, what do I do?"

"I really like Reed," Ophelia says slowly, "but are you sure he deserves a second—or a third or whatever number he's up to —chance?"

"I was upset last night because, well, I was feeling tender about my birthday. It's the anniversary of my dad walking out."

"Fuck, I'm so sorry, Lani." Nicole looks guilt stricken. "I should have listened to you about your birthday."

"You didn't know because I didn't tell you. I've kept a lot of myself from you guys and I'm trying to change. So I was emotional, and Reed and I finally had the fight we should have had six years ago. And yes, he hasn't made all the right moves, but he's apologized, and I still—I love him."

What happens if, after all of this, Reed and I can't bridge the miles, or the years? What if I've lost the love of my life because I was too stubborn? "I think I need to go there. I need to go to New York."

"Lani Kalama wants to follow a man someplace?" Kate's astonishment shows in her quirked eyebrows.

"Do you know what I wished for on my stupid birthday candles? I wished that we belonged together, that we belonged to each other. If I truly want that, I have to make room for him in my life. I didn't fight for him back then. I need to fight for him now."

"You win, Lani, in the grand gestures department," Ophelia says with a wave of her hand. "I only had to say 'I love you' in front of fifty people. You're going to have to fly three thousand miles and track Reed down in one of the biggest cities on the planet."

"Or I can call him and get his address," I say.

She grins. "Or that."

"So you don't think I'm a bad feminist?"

"Sweetheart, you're fighting for what you want. It doesn't matter if it's a job, or a house, or a guy. You're making the life you deserve."

"Thanks."

I look to Nicole. "Is it okay if I take a few days off?"

"You are hereby banned from the office until you get this mess sorted out."

"Oh shit, the house inspection. It's scheduled for Tuesday. I can't miss it."

Silence falls as we contemplate the delay of my grand gesture.

Ever sensible Rosie pats my shoulder. "Look, you and Reed have managed to overcome a lot. You can overcome a few more days apart."

"Right. Sure." My skin crawls with the need to get this fixed. But Reed is not a manufacturing problem I'm going to attack and solve. He is a person who has hurt me and who I've hurt right back. But it's not a competition. We can only win if we stop playing games once and for all.

CHAPTER 33

Sunday

LANI

Hi. Not sure if you got my earlier text. I got your note. And the check. Thank you.

I was thinking maybe we could talk? If you want.

I'm assuming you're in New York.

I want to apologize and I don't want to do it by text.

But I'll also understand if you don't want to talk.

LANI

OK. I get the message.

Monday

REED

Hey

I've been on deadline. Haven't been checking my messages, sorry.

I have to get this book to my editor by Fri

Everything OK?

LANI

Sorry, I was in a meeting. I don't want to distract you from your deadline. Maybe call me when you have time?

Tuesday

1 MISSED CALL FROM REED BENNET

LANI

Sorry I missed your call. I was at the house inspection.

Try me again if you want.

Wednesday

OPHELIA

Hi Reed. My students have written you the most precious thank-you notes for coming to read to them. Can you give me your address so I can mail them to you?

REED

Hi Ophelia. That's so nice. Can you send them to my agent? I'm moving and wouldn't want them to get lost.

Oh? Can I ask where to?

Not sure yet.

I know it's not my business, but we were sort of hoping you'd be coming back to SB. Is that happening?

I have to say, I'm surprised. I figured you all would hate me.

We don't hate you, Reed. We all like you a lot. You kind of slotted right into the group.

I did?

We miss you. So let us know when you're back in town.

There's a lot up in the air right now.

But if I do come back to SB, I will let you know if you like.

Please do.

* * *

OPHELIA

I was only able to get his agent's info. Reed says he's moving but didn't say where.

LANI

Send it to me, please.

Thanks, you're the best. 

Thursday

REED

I just sent you the latest version. Look at it. Please tell me you don't want any changes.

KINGSTON

Looking now

You did it, man. Reed and Lucy Go to School is going to be another bestseller. Koko's going to flip for it.

You think?

I know

Thanks. Turn it in for me? I'm going to sleep for a week.

I'm proud of you, Reed.

I think it's a good note to go out on.

You're still thinking you want to pull the plug on Reed and Lucy?

I don't think I can do it anymore. Not with things the way they are.

Let's talk—how about brunch Saturday?

OK

Friday

1 MISSED CALL FROM LANI KALAMA

1 MISSED CALL FROM REED BENNET

KINGSTON

Brunch still on? Meet me at the carousel in Prospect Park at 10 tomorrow.

REED

That is oddly specific, but as I have no other life, I'll be there.

Saturday

LANI

Hi Reed. Sorry for the phone tag. Did you get the book turned in?

REED

Hi! Yes. It was a big push, but it's finally with my editor.

Is now a good time to talk?

Actually, I'm on my way to brunch with Kingston.

I could call you after?

Sure.

CHAPTER 34
REED

Fall colors are beginning to tinge the trees in Prospect Park, as if a giant holding a paintbrush had tramped through overnight, dripping crimson and yellow ochre onto the leaves. I've got on a denim jacket in a nod to the cooler air. This is honestly the most beautiful time to be in New York, when the humidity of summer dries up and the deep cold of late autumn is a ways off. I'd like to remember the city like this, a version in which I could have been happy.

Suddenly, tears prick at my eyes. I've been lonely in New York before, but somehow my loneliness seems more profound since I got back from California.

The first time we broke up, I gradually realized Lani wasn't coming to Iowa, that we weren't going to bend for each other. We were at an impasse, and in the end, I accepted that we wanted different things and let her go. Now I see what an absurd choice I made, yet I can't completely regret it, because it forced me to grow up and see the world as it is, not as I want it to be.

But this time, this so-called clean break, hurts ten times more. I lived the dream for a handful of days. I had a glimpse of what we could be like if we let each other in. Now I have to live with knowing what could have been.

Lani has been trying to reach me all week, and we've had trouble connecting. The irony is not lost on me. I haven't been terribly excited about finally having the conversation she wants to have. I'm not eager to hear her plans for formally ending our marriage—the one tie we have left to each other.

But that's just me, wanting the world to conform to my romantic ideas, wanting to write a different ending to our story. The real world isn't going to give me Lani on a platter. I had my chance.

I stop my pathetic internal monologue when I reach the carousel and catch sight of a familiar person in the clusters of parkgoers. I was expecting Kingston, but he's not the one standing there, scanning the crowd. It's Lani.

She's wearing a little brown hat over her straight black hair, a chic rust-colored coat belted around her slim waist. A saffron-colored bag hangs over one shoulder. She looks like an autumn leaf blown to the ground.

She doesn't see me right away, so I have time to internally freak out. What is she doing here? Has someone died? Have *I* died and the carousel in Prospect Park is my heaven?

Or is she here to flatten me by serving me with divorce papers in person?

Maybe this is hell.

My phone buzzes and I look down. I have a text.

KINGSTON

So it turns out I can't make brunch. Raincheck tomorrow?

I ignore this because Kingston is clearly a lying liar who lies, but when I look up, Lani is gone. Maybe I imagined her and I'm still reeling from sleep deprivation after late nights working on the book.

Then I hear my name. "Reed."

"Lani?"

She's standing a couple of feet away and waves with a hand clad in a burgundy suede glove. She looks like a California girl guessing how to dress for a different climate. I don't think she's ever been farther east than Nevada. She looks beautiful, and overly warm. It's probably sixty-five degrees.

"What are you doing here?"

"I came to see you."

"Everything okay at home?" The words leave my mouth awkwardly. Whose home am I talking about? I wish it were mine, but it's not. Not yet. "In Santa Barbara, I mean."

"Santa Barbara is fine. I had the house inspection a few days ago and everything looks good. The inspector says the house has good bones. That's encouraging, right?"

"Positively. You're getting a great house." But why are we talking about the house, when it still makes no sense that Lani is in Prospect Park instead of on State Street. "I can't believe you're here. Like, really here. I never thought..." Suddenly it sinks in. She's come all this way, on an airplane, tracked me down at the park, apparently convinced Kingston to be her ally, and she looks darling in her fall fashion. She didn't come all this way to serve me divorce papers.

My chest feels like it's been pumped full of helium. "You followed me."

She looks guilty, as if I've caught her doing something illicit. "Yes."

"Why are you here, Lani?"

CHAPTER 35

LANI

Why am I here? I know the answer, but the words are stuck in my throat.

I've gotten this far on pure adrenaline. Since confirming with Kingston that he turned in the Reed and Lucy book, I've been going nonstop, booking my flight, arranging with Ophelia to water my plants, making sure work was wrapped enough to leave Nicole to her own devices for a few days. I packed a bag and flew to the opposite side of the country. I've flown to and from Hawaii dozens of times, but I've never flown to the East Coast.

The three-hour time difference makes my head feel strange, and the city air, cool but smelling of smoke and exhaust, doesn't help clear it. Noise comes from all sides and there are people absolutely everywhere. New York is life cranked up to eleven, while Santa Barbara is a steady seven, and Hawaii a mellow four.

But walking with Reed through this Technicolor-green park, I feel like I could stay here forever, as long as he's with me.

My throat unsticks and the first thing I blurt out is, "I made a mistake."

"About what?" Reed asks carefully.

"About a lot of things. When you left for Iowa, I didn't follow you because I was angry and scared. I wish I had."

"You do?" He looks surprised.

"And then at my birthday party, I was upset and tired and you were right that I was lying to myself about what I really wanted. I regret lashing out at you and I'm sorry."

"Thanks, but you had a right to. I can't believe it took me so long to apologize for what happened way back then."

"See, the thing is, I think we both have some growing up to do. But that's okay. We're not perfect. I think that if we stick together, we can help each other be better."

"Stick together?"

"You know, for better and for worse." I sneak a glance up at him, and he's smiling.

"For richer, for poorer?" he says softly. He stops walking and takes my hands in his. I wish I weren't wearing gloves so I could feel his skin against mine.

"In sickness and in health," I say, looking into his cloud-gray eyes.

"Till death do us part?"

"That's the general idea." I pull my hands away and rummage around in my shoulder bag until one hand closes around a leather pouch. I fumble it open, shake the simple gold band out and onto the palm of my glove.

"You found it."

"I knew where it was the whole time."

Reed chuckles, then his hand goes to his neck. He fishes a chain out from under his shirt. Hanging from the end is a matching gold band. "Same."

I laugh. We're a pair of lovestruck fools. "So are we going to do this? The most epic do-over in history?"

"You want to skip right to being married?"

"Well, I was sort of hoping we could have a honeymoon period," I say, exaggeratedly batting my eyelashes.

He laughs. "I'm on board with that. But first." He takes the ring from my palm, then pulls my gloves off one at a time, sticking them back in my coat pocket. His fingers trail over the knuckles on my left hand. My breath stutters. The ring fits perfectly, winking softly in the slanted sunlight.

I return the gesture when he slips the chain over his head and removes his ring. It feels heavy in my palm, the weight of our promise to each other made real. His nails are cut square, his fingers thick and dear to me. I push the ring over his knuckle, sliding it home.

Home. He's my home and I'm his.

He kisses me then, a happy kiss, warm and hopeful. I wind my arms around his neck, keeping him close, pouring my love into kissing him back.

We finally stop for air. I tuck myself into his side, feeling satisfied when he puts his arm securely around my waist and we begin to walk away from the carousel crowd, down one of the park's many footpaths.

"So, are your roommates home?" I ask.

"Fuck if I know. I avoid the place."

"Where do you work?"

"Usually the library. Sometimes a coffee shop. Occasionally Kingston's living room."

"Oh yes, the famous Kingston. Think I could meet him while I'm here?"

"How long are you here for?"

"As long as you want me."

"Forever, Lani. I want you forever. But I know you have your job to get back to, and your house, and your friends. Your life."

"I want you to be in my life."

"I want that, too. New York, as we've established, isn't for me."

"And Santa Barbara is?"

"It could be. But if you want me to move to Goleta or Ventura just for kicks, I will."

"That's not necessary. Besides, we had a bargain: you always have a place to stay when you come into town."

"Yes, I do remember our agreement." He strokes his chin and in a deadpan voice says, "Your guest room will make a great base while I apartment hunt."

"Actually, I was hoping you might consider cohabitation with me. In my room. My house. Our house, actually."

"You want me to move in with you?"

"Well, it would be inefficient to try to maintain a marriage across town. Also, I love you, by the way, and I'm done posturing. Yes, I want to live together. Besides, the house is going to need some work, so I figure you'll be useful to have around."

He lifts his eyebrows. "Oh yeah? You think I can be handy around the house?"

"Well, at least you can let the plumber and the electrician in if I'm at work."

"Fair point." He stops, pulls me to the side of the path so we don't get run over by the eternal tide of city dwellers. "And don't think I missed the little nugget buried in your 'let's live together' monologue."

"I don't know what you're talking about," I say airily.

"You said you love me."

"Oh, that." I drop the act and smile. "I do."

His gaze moves to my mouth and he groans. "Shit. Yeah, let's find a bed. We need to consummate our love immediately. Maybe we should get a hotel room."

"Actually, I do have a room around the corner from your apartment."

"How do you know where I live? Oh. Kingston."

"I may have convinced him to give me some information in the name of true love."

"Thank God he's a romantic."

"Yes, he was very helpful. So, hotel?"

"Hotel."

We ride the subway hand in hand, and every time we make eye contact we have to smother giggles like it's our first date. We're not new to each other, but everything feels like the first time all over again.

The hotel is simple and clean and empty except for the usual furniture and my rolling carry-on.

I'm about to ask if Reed wants anything, not that I can offer him much besides bottled water or the emergency protein bar at the bottom of my purse, but as soon as the door locks behind us, he's got me pressed up against it, his entire large, substantial body on me, a wall of hotness.

His legs frame mine, I'm slotted right up against the vee of his jeans, and I'm wearing far too many layers. Even though his mouth is on mine, Reed seems to be able to read my mind. He takes off my frivolous little hat first, then goes for my belt. He's relentless, never letting me up for air, and I'm here for it, gladly drowning in his kisses, smelling nothing but him, barely registering when he slides my coat down my arms, pulls my mustard-colored blouse free from my pleated skirt.

He lifts his head, murmurs something that sounds like "autumn leaf," but that can't be right. The thought falls away as soon as his thumbs brush my nipples through my thin lace bra. My nipples stand to attention and he doesn't disappoint them, stroking and squeezing until I'm squirming against him so hard I can feel his insistent erection through all these layers of fabric.

I could stand here and be plundered by his tongue for eternity, but I suppose I should do some of the work. I wriggle out of his grasp long enough to unzip my ankle boots and kick them off. Off go my tights and skirt. The blouse follows, and I crawl onto the bed in my panties and bra. I'm never certain how often the duvet covers in hotels are laundered, so I strip this one off to get to the clean white sheets beneath.

Reed's been watching me the whole time, but when I pat the space beside me he goes into high gear. In a flash he's in bed next to me, naked except for his leather bracelet and the ring on his finger that I put there for a second time just an hour ago.

It's not like we didn't do this a couple of weeks ago, but it's still different from the sex I'm used to. And this time is even more intense than the last, because we know we're both in love, and I'm not going to let him go anywhere I can't follow this time.

"I missed you," I say, because it's true. I've missed him since the moment I drove away from the restaurant the night of my birthday party. And before that, when he was in Los Angeles, and before that, when he was in a different state and the only way I could feel close to him was by reading Reed and Lucy books and remembering the good times.

"I missed you so much," he says, gathering me into his arms. We're mostly naked, and he's flushed and hard, and I'm slippery wet between my legs, but this embrace isn't about sex. It's about needing to feel we're actually in the same place for once—physically, emotionally, and mentally.

"I'm glad you want to move to California," I say. "It might have been a pain to convince Nicole to open a New York office of Winesap Design."

"What are you talking about?"

"I don't want to be where you aren't. I've had it with pretending I don't want something just because I think other people don't think I should want it."

"Are you saying you'd move here to be with me?"

I think about it for a minute. I could qualify it, to make myself seem harder, stronger, more independent. But it really comes down to—

"Yes."

"Wow." He sits up and faces me. "That means a lot, Lani. I'm one lucky son of a bitch. I'm not going to fuck this up, I swear."

"Hey, I'm not asking you to be perfect. We're probably both going to make mistakes. But if we're together, I think we can get through them."

"I don't want to miss you ever again," he says, his eyes soft and serious.

I can't help but kiss him. His mouth is warm and immediately causes me to lose my train of thought. A little later, I'm underneath him, my underwear long gone. He's inside me, with a thumb on my clit, and I'm coming so hard my brains feel like they're being scrambled with pleasure. "Reed, I love you," I hear myself say as if from very far away, and he groans out my name as he comes inside me, deep and long.

"Lani?" he says, his head resting on my heart, his fingers dancing along the skin of my arm, making me quiver in anticipation of round two.

"Hmmm?"

"Let's go home."

CHAPTER 36

REED

Of course, actually moving isn't as simple as grabbing my wife and packing a bag and heading west on the first airplane out of Dodge.

For one thing, Kingston. My phone buzzes at eight on the dot the next morning. Lani, who is on California time, barely moves, but I accidentally hit answer instead of silence, and get Kingston booming in my ear about breakfast and Koko and the new contract and I hiss at him that I'll be at the diner in thirty minutes if he'll only stop talking right this second.

Lani sits up sleepily, the silk strap of the camisole she'd eventually put on in the night slipping over her shoulder. "What's going on?"

We'd ventured out once for a quick dinner of Thai food and otherwise spent the entire rest of yesterday making love and whispering embarrassingly sweet nothings to each other. Couldn't have been time better spent.

But the problem I've always faced is that life isn't like a book, where you can skip over the boring parts and only get to the major turning points. I struggle into the clothes I was wearing yesterday. "I have to meet Kingston."

"Oh." She blinks like a movie star whose beauty sleep has been interrupted. "Can I come?"

"You're super tired, it's like 5 a.m. your time."

"It's okay. I want to meet Kingston. And coffee."

"Coffee. Okay."

We're only a few minutes late, Lani dressed as casually as I've ever seen her in yoga pants and an off-the shoulder T-shirt, army-style jacket, and big hoop earrings. I smile privately. Did she pack what she thought would be New York-appropriate clothes?

Kingston is sitting at the same table we shared a week ago, when I was hungover and heartbroken and ready to throw everything away.

"Hey, man," I say. He's looking chipper for a Sunday morning, dressed down for him in a paisley shirt and painted-on jeans, his dreds swept back in a ponytail tied with a silk scarf that matches the paisley. I feel grimy in yesterday's clothes, and I haven't showered or shaved, though before we left the hotel room I scrubbed my teeth with a toothpaste-coated finger.

Kingston looks at me, then at Lani, then back to me. His smirk grows into a grin. "Good morning, party people."

"Kingston James, meet Lani Kalama."

She smiles confidently and offers him her hand. "So great to meet you at last. Thanks for all the help."

"Delighted, my dear," he says, shaking her hand. "It's an honor to meet Lucy—I mean, Lani." He tries to look bashful, but I know the slip was intentional.

I pull out Lani's chair and then my own. "Yes, well, we require coffee."

The server comes by and when we're appropriately caffeinated, we all sit and stare at each other.

"So," Lani tries. "You're a book agent. Do you enjoy that?"

"Sometimes," Kingston says. "It helps when your clients aren't nuts." He gives me a pointed look. "But when they produce award-winning, best-selling books, you have to give them a little slack. Which reminds me, does the presence of Miss Kalama mean you're over your drama about walking away from the Reed and Lucy series?"

I cringe. I'd forgotten how melodramatic I was being in the midst of the deadline and facing the possibility of a lifetime without the woman I loved.

"Walking away from Reed and Lucy? What is he talking about, Reed?" Lani sounds alarmed.

Before I can answer, Kingston cuts in. "Oh, just that the last time we were sitting in these very seats he said something about feeling guilty for mining your relationship for the characters' dynamic and not being a real writer and giving it all up."

"To be fair, I was incredibly hungover." The ghost of that hangover seems to hover over the table as we speak. I take a prophylactic sip of coffee and when the server comes back I order plenty of bacon, my hangover cure, to be on the safe side, though since I found Lani in the park I haven't had so much as a drop of alcohol.

"You were going to stop writing Reed and Lucy because of me?" Lani asks softly when the server is gone.

I struggle with how to answer. "It didn't feel right. I only started writing those characters as a way to cope with being soul-crushingly lonely. Reed and Lucy made me feel less alone. And then I saw you again and I realized I'd been living this half-life for so long, the only good thing in it was leftovers from our life together. Not to mention, I thought I was going to write great novels and here I am writing children's books with five hundred words in them. It doesn't make sense for me to keep living in the past. I wouldn't be able to move forward that way."

"But so many people love Reed and Lucy," Lani says. "Including me. You have to keep writing them. You're going to need something to work on in your studio."

"What studio?"

"In the house. If you want. I have it all planned out. We're going to gut the pantry and push it out over the deck. That'll give you room for a drafting table for your drawings, and we can put in a desk on the other wall for your computer."

"You thought about this?"

"I've been thinking about it for a while. Ever since you showed up in my life again, I've been fantasizing about ways to keep you there."

"You have?" I slip her hand into mine and raise it to my mouth. My lips brush over the gold band on her ring finger.

Kingston clears his throat noisily. I look up. I forgot he was there.

"Maybe this would be a good time to mention that Koko loved the draft of *Reed and Lucy Go to School* so much she told me she wants to wrap up the terms of the contract extension ASAP. Three more books, new terms. More favorable, naturally, but you leave all that to me."

I look at Lani, my lodestone. "What do you think?"

"I think if you really don't want to write Reed and Lucy anymore you could make a success of another project, but I'd be sad if their adventures were over."

She's right. I do have more Reed and Lucy adventures to share with the world. "I was actually thinking about starting a new series for older readers. Reed and Lucy have to grow up sometime."

"*Reed and Lucy Grow Up*. I like the sound of that," Lani says.

"After all, my readers will get older. This would give them somewhere to go."

"And there's no law that says you can't work on multiple projects at the same time, is there? You can add to the Reed and Lucy series, and also write for older readers. Why not write a novel, too?"

I look at Lani and wonder if this can really be my life now. She believes in me. I know that now. And being around her feels like it's unlocking something inside of me that's held me back for too long.

I turn back to Kingston. "In other words, you're going to be very busy cutting deals for all these new projects. Yes, let's get the contract signed."

"That's what I'm talking about," he says with a smile. "Let's drink to your continued success."

To seal the deal, the three of us clink our porcelain mugs in a greasy spoon toast.

"Agent hat off," he says, miming removing a hat and setting it on the table. "Friend hat on. Now I want to hear about what the heck is going on with you two. Playing happy families again?"

Lani's cheeks get a little pink. God, she's adorable.

"I'm officially leaving New York, as soon as I can. Lani has generously invited me to move in with her."

"We may be an unconventional married couple, but I don't think we need to maintain separate residences," she says.

"Married? You mean—"

I hold up my hand to show off my ring, right where it should be. Kingston glows harder.

"Damn. Where should I send the place setting?"

"No gifts, please." Lani laughs. "My friends will probably want to have some kind of party. That's what they do. And you'll definitely be invited."

"I guess I can put in an appearance. I do like West Coast style."

"You'll fit right in."

"Well, I'm happy for you guys. And Lani, I salute you for taking this guy off my hands."

"Hey," I protest. "I'm not that bad."

They both smile at me as if I'm a cute toddler and I bristle. "Seriously. I'm a grown-up."

Kingston laughs and the server brings us plates of steaming

food. Later, when I'm full of bacon and floating on a coffee high, Kingston says, "Time to start brainstorming for the next three Reed and Lucy books. *Reed and Lucy Go to Divorce Court* is out, so how about *Reed and Lucy Go to the Empire State Building*? You could research it before you fly back."

"I'd prefer *Reed and Lucy Go to the Statue of Liberty*," Lani says. "I've always wanted to see it."

"*Reed and Lucy Go to Tiffany*," I offer. Lani looks at me with surprise. "What? I want to get you an engagement ring. I never did, the first time."

"Isn't that a bit backward?" she asks. "Considering I already have a wedding ring?"

"Girl, don't turn down a trip to Tiffany. What are you thinking?" Kingston asks, hand over his heart.

Lani yawns. "You're right. Reed and Lani will go to Tiffany right after we go back to bed."

"Reed and Lani go to bed, I'll sign off on that," I say.

Kingston makes a face. "You two lovebirds go have your married people sex, and I'll take care of the bill. Business expense and all."

Lani leans over and gives Kingston a kiss on the cheek. "Thanks, Kingston, for taking care of him, being there for him. I appreciate it."

"You're welcome, Lani. Good luck. You're going to need it."

She laughs, tinkling and sweet. "Thanks. We'll be fine."

I give Kingston a tight hug. I know I'll see him again before I leave, but this still feels like something of a goodbye. Perhaps it's simply the end of a chapter, this part of my life that I wouldn't have survived without him. "Thanks, man. I—" There's so much to thank him for, and I can't find the right words. "I'm grateful."

"Hey, I'm happy for you. And I'm proud of you for not giving up."

"Couldn't have done it without you."

"I know." He winks. "Now scoot. I'm late for a date with a handsome dog walker I literally tripped over."

"I like him," Lani says as we're checking out of her hotel, before making our way to my apartment to begin packing. "He reminds me of someone. But who?"

"I hate to break it to you, but he's kind of my Nicole."

She claps her hands over her eyes. "Oh no. There are two of them."

"Yes, aren't we lucky?" I ask.

She beams up at me and my heart aches with happiness. "Yes, aren't we."

You're invited to an open house to celebrate our new
home!

Saturday, December 19
5PM–10PM

Festive dress
No gifts

Lani Kalama & Reed Bennet

EPILOGUE
LANI

I'm putting the finishing touches on a giant green salad, wondering what else I've forgotten in the mad rush to get this housewarming/Christmas/we're-staying-married party off the ground.

It took us barely a week to get Reed's life in New York all packed up and sent to California. We spent the time until we closed on the house working and making plans for the renovations. By a stroke of luck, the contractor I'd already worked with once before on the expansion at Winesap Design became available at the last minute, and his crew worked for four weeks straight to get the studio perfect, the deck repairs done, and the light bathroom remodels finished, too.

We moved in a week ago, and Nicole made us throw a party to celebrate. I might have wanted to show off my new house and my new (old) husband, as well.

Rosie and Gus are the first to arrive, as well as the first to flout the "no gifts" request. Gus bears a gorgeous houseplant in a pretty terra-cotta pot.

"It's a *Dracaena draco*," he says. "Easy to maintain."

"And if you want to, you can plant it in your yard and in about thirty years it'll be as big as a car," Rosie explains.

"Good to know." I find a home for it with some of my other plants while Gus gives me a quick rundown of care.

Rosie glows in a pretty rose-red dress. "Need any help?"

There's another knock on the door and I head that way, calling over my shoulder, "You can help yourselves to drinks."

Ophelia and Jamie stand on the doorstep arm in arm, his dark hair and her blonde both a little askew, a trace of what looks like lipstick on Jamie's chin. I suppress a smile. They think they're subtle, but they so aren't.

"We know you said no gifts." Ophelia pushes her way in and hands me a tissue-paper-wrapped rectangle. "But it's a first edition of my favorite children's book. *Miss Rumphius.*"

"Barbara Cooney," Reed says, appearing at my side. "She's one of my favorites. Thank you so much."

"And later I want to talk to you about doing a reading at our museum fundraiser," Jamie reminds Reed.

"Absolutely. Drink?"

"Sure." Reed points Jamie in the direction of our built-in bar, an original fixture of the house we thought was too cool to mess with.

The door opens again and I'm beginning to think I should leave it wide open. "Kate, Oliver, hey!"

I take Kate's coat, and my eyes grow wide at the size of her belly. "Yikes, Kate, please do not go into labor at my party."

"I'm trying to hold him in there," she promises. "But maybe I should sit down."

Oliver thrusts a covered casserole dish into my hands, then rushes to help Kate into one of the matching aquamarine brocade armchairs Reed and I picked out together on State Street a few weeks ago.

"It's a thing of Brussels sprouts from the restaurant. Do you want something to drink, sweetheart?" Without waiting for her to answer he says, "I'm going to get you some water."

Kate grimaces. "He gets worse the closer to the due date we get."

"Thanks for the Brussels sprouts," I say to Oliver's retreating back. He doesn't acknowledge me, intent on his mission to keep Kate comfortable.

Reed opens the door to the next arrival. "Kingston!" There's much manly backslapping, and I get in a hug, too.

"I can't wait for you to meet everyone," I say. "What's that?"

"Champagne, obviously." Kingston hands the chilled bottle to me with ceremony. "This is a celebration, is it not?"

"I don't know why we even bothered," I mutter. "Yes, we are most definitely celebrating, and thank you."

I set the bottle down on the bar and turn back to take Kingston's camel-colored overcoat, when another knock sounds at the door.

"We're not late, I hope?" Nicole swans her way in, then stops and stares at Kingston. She's wearing a nearly identical coat and carrying a bottle of chilled champagne. "Hello."

"Nicole, this is Kingston. Kingston, this is Nicole." I take a step back. This will either be an uncomfortable showdown, or they'll soon be plotting world domination together. "Hi, Ricky."

"Hi, Lani." Ricky gives me a hug and shakes Reed's hand. "Thanks for having us."

"Thanks for coming." My head's spinning with love for every single person in this cozy house. I invited a few people from work, and some of our old friends that Reed and I are trying to get back in touch with. But none of them are on the other side of the door when the next knock sounds.

"Mom! Oh my God! I didn't think you were coming."

"Reed found a last-minute deal on a flight and he said I should come!"

I hug her tightly. I spot Reed behind her and give him a look. "Oh he did?"

"Surprise," he says, grinning.

"This is so incredible." It feels kind of amazing to have pretty much everyone I love under one roof.

"Here's your early Christmas present." Mom hands me a familiar-shaped tin.

"Macadamia nuts, yay!" I hide them in the kitchen instead of putting them on the buffet table. What? Everyone needs a vice.

There's much buzzing and talking and clinking of glasses as everyone gets their preferred beverage. I hear the pop of a champagne cork and notice Nicole and Kingston with their heads tilted together, already thick as thieves. Reed materializes at my shoulder, handing me a glass of red wine.

"Should we make a toast?" he asks, squeezing my hand.

"I suppose. It's all so wonderful." I can't help the buoyant feeling in my chest or the sappy smile that's surely adorning my face.

"You're wonderful," he says, kissing me on the cheek. "I love you so much."

"I love you, too." Every time I say it makes me want to say it more.

"Your attention, please," I call. The room quiets down after a beat, eyes turning to look at me and Reed. "Thank you all for coming. Mom, I can't believe you're here. Kingston, thanks for flying all this way. My fellow Never a Brides, and my favorite bride of all." Nicole winks and I smile. "You guys are my family, and Reed and I are so lucky to have you in our lives."

"We're lucky to have you," Nicole breaks in.

"Thanks. So welcome to our home. Merry Christmas. Happy holidays. And Reed." I turn to him and raise my glass. "You're the love of my life, my husband, my best friend." The tears catch in my throat and I swallow thickly. "And I'm honored to be your wife."

"Hear, hear," someone calls. I hear a few sniffles amidst the clinking of glasses.

"Lani, my heart, my soul. My wife. My everything. I'm the luckiest guy in the world. I love you."

More awwing and cheering, and then someone starts a whisper campaign of "kiss, kiss, kiss."

So we do.

* * *

Thank you so much for reading *Can't Hurry Love*. Read on for *Can't Hardly Wait*, a bonus story featuring everyone's favorite bride, Nicole!

If you loved the Never a Bride series, you will enjoy my Sawyer's Cove: The Reboot series, which starts with a prequel starring Kate from *Can't Fight This Feeling*! Scan the code to download for free!

xoxo,

Libby

CAN'T HARDLY WAIT

A NEVER A BRIDE STORY

From the diary of Nicole Winesap, age 9

My birthday's in five days and I really really really want pierced ears. Mom says I can when I turn ten, but I've been trying to tell her that nine is almost as old as ten and every other girl in my class has pierced ears anyway, even though that's not exactly true but close enough. I worked on her all the way home from soccer today and she didn't say I could yet, but I'm not giving up.

She and Dad had another fight after dinner tonight. I guess Dad's been working so much and Mom says she never sees him, which is kind of weird because his office is like a mile away and a lot of my friends' dad's work all the way in L.A. and only come home on weekends. I think maybe Mom is just bored.

When I grow up, I'm never getting married. Married people fight and never get to do anything fun. I can't wait until college so I can get out of Santa Barbara and go somewhere different. Like New York! Oh my gosh, the sixth-grade class just got back from their trip there and they said it was so amazing. They even got to see a Broadway show!

All I do is wait. Five days until my birthday. A whole year until I get my ears pierced, maybe. Two more years until my turn to take a class trip to New York. I can't wait until I'm grown up and I can do whatever I want whenever I want.

* * *

NOTES PASSED BETWEEN RICKY KENDELL, AGE 9, AND HIS COUSIN JAMIE KENDELL, AGE 7

> Girls are so gross! Lacey Torres gave me a big pink heart valentine at school and I tore it into a hundred pieces and put in the trash.

> Yuck. Is she your girlfriend now?

> I guess so.

* * *

FROM THE JOURNAL OF NICOLE WINESAP, AGE 16

Well, it's done. After months of orchestrating our first date, I finally got Murphy to kiss me tonight.

It wasn't exactly how I'd pictured it. In the movies, the couple always seems to fit together like two puzzle pieces, but this was kind of awkward? He's like at least a foot taller than me, so I had to stand on my tiptoes and he had to kind of scrunch down, and his lips were like, really dry? Is that normal? And he tasted like burritos.

At least I can finally say I've had my first kiss. And Murphy is super sweet. Plus, he's going to NYU next year, so if I get in, too, I'd know someone there already. Not that I think we're going to stay together or anything. I wonder if college guys kiss better than high school boys????

Maybe sex is better than kissing?

Only one way to find out.

* * *

FROM THE JOURNAL OF NICOLE WINESAP, AGE 18

College is the absolute best! I thought UCLA was going to be so annoying and just like high school (I still can't believe my parents refused to let me even apply to NYU—I may never forgive them for that) but it's actually been fantastic. There are tons of cute guys in all my classes, and I've already made two girlfriends. I thought the girls here would already be in cliques from high school, but pretty much everyone on my hall is really nice. Rosie's so shy I feel like the prom queen next to her, and Kate's tons of fun and already has the campus mapped out because she grew up near here, so I'm already feeling at home.

Rosie's pre-med, because she's a genius, but at least Kate and I have some classes together. We had Econ today, and it wasn't bad. The first few weeks are basically review, so that's easy enough.

That reminds me—there was a ~~cute~~ interesting guy in Econ. I saw him looking at me a couple of times. I suppose he could have been looking at Kate—it remains to be seen how smart it was to make friends with someone hotter than me—but I sort of felt like he was looking at me. He's not my type at all—very straitlaced. Conservative, even. But there was something about the way he looked at me—shivers. And not in a creepy way, I swear. Anyway. I'll have to find out his name next week.

Gotta run to the art library, then there's an honest-to-god toga party off campus that Kate knows about. College rules!

* * *

TEXTS BETWEEN RICKY KENDELL, AGE 18, AND JAMIE KENDELL, AGE 16

RICKY

College girls are a million times hotter than high school girls, Jamie. You have to come visit.

JAMIE

What happens between senior year of high school and freshman year of college? Hot girl alchemy?

Smartass. Just come down this weekend.

I'll see if I can borrow Dad's car.

You hooked up with any of them yet?

I met the woman I'm going to marry, that's all.

What's her name?

I don't know yet. She's in my Econ class.

Mysterious. Just like the invisible hand.

Shut up.

* * *

FROM THE JOURNAL OF NICOLE WINESAP, AGE 18

So it turns out that guy from Econ's name is Ricky—what a dorky name, right? I think it's short for Richard. Why not Rich? Anyway, it turns out he's actually from Santa Barbara too, but even though I thought I'd met every rich, no pun intended, kid in the city, we never crossed paths because he went to Laguna Blanca, while I went to Cate, obviously. His dad has some investment fund thing, of course.

How did I find all this out, when in the six weeks we've had Econ together he's never once spoken to me? We got put together to work on a group project—him, me, and some dance major who's clearly only taking this class to get a social science credit. I have a feeling Ricky and I are going to be doing most of the work on this one.

Anyway, we met up after class to talk about the project and before I knew it, we'd walked all the way to Dykstra, talking the whole way. He is about as conservative as I thought at first, with his polos and his Young Republican haircut, but he was really nice, and, I don't know... he's a freshman, too, so we're the same age, but he talked to me like we were both adults, not barely post-adolescent.

It was—I don't know.

I guess he wants to go into finance, gag me. At least it's not real estate like my dad. But he seems really into all the wonky theory stuff which is kind of cute. Not cute, cute. Whatever. We're meeting tomorrow after lunch to go over the project.

On a completely unrelated note, maybe I'll wear my new jeans.

* * *

TEXTS BETWEEN RICKY KENDELL, AGE 20, AND JAMIE KENDELL, AGE 18

JAMIE

You made a move on your future wife yet?

RICKY

Still biding my time.

Aren't you worried someone else is going to scoop her up?

Not really. She's too independent to be scooped.

So what makes you different?

When it comes to her, I'll wait forever.

* * *

FROM THE JOURNAL OF NICOLE WINESAP, AGE 20

I'm floating on a cloud right now. It's ten at night and I'm practically shaking as I write this down. Two years of just being friends and dating other people and barely crossing paths some semesters and *Ricky Fucking Kendell* just kissed me.

I wasn't even planning to see him tonight. I went to the library to get a book for my Lit class and he was there, too. He asked me if I was going to walk home alone and I said yes and he said no, he'd walk me, because that's what he does. He's a gentleman, as well I know, because he always looks me in the eye when we talk instead of staring at my breasts like half the straight guys on this campus. So I said okay and then we walked back and it reminded me of that first time we walked across campus together as freshman and I told him so and he stopped and looked at me kind of funny.

He said, "You remember that?"

Maybe I wasn't supposed to, but I said, "Of course I do."

And he didn't say anything for a while and then he asked me if I was still dating Travis and I said that was old news and I asked if he was still seeing that girl I saw him with at Homecoming and he said she was just a friend.

"You have a lot of friends who are girls?" I asked him.

"A few."

I think I was a little mad then because he's never made a move on me in two years and even though it was always kind of nice that I could count on him to be there without hitting on me the fact that he never did always rubbed me the wrong way.

I said, "Is that your thing? Friends with benefits? Never actually dating anyone?" Not like I'm the poster child for monogamy, but right then it wasn't about me.

"Not exactly," he said. "There's no point in dating if you don't see a future with someone."

And I got it. He never hit on me because I wasn't the type of girl he could see a future with. I got really mad then. "So you just hook up with girls you wouldn't even bring home to your mother?" I didn't really mean it. And I know he's not really like that—I'd have heard about it if he was.

But he surprised me. He said, "I don't hook up at all."

That took a minute to process. "What, like—you're a—" I couldn't quite make myself say the word virgin, but it was implied.

"I know it's old-fashioned, but I've been waiting for the right woman."

I think I said something really dumb like, "That's so brave." Something idiotic. Because I've slept with... counting, give me a minute... *eleven* guys since Murphy and it never occurred to me there were college juniors, especially junior boys, who still have their v-card.

"So, what, you're waiting for your soulmate or something? Aren't you worried you won't find her?"

"No, I found her already. I'm just waiting for her to be ready for me."

And there was something in his voice. I swear I was

blushing like a fire engine. Because when he said that, I felt, I knew, what he meant. He meant—

And then he touched my chin and tilted it up—he's a couple of inches taller than me—and he was so sweet and so serious and it was the most mortifying but also the most romantic thing that's ever happened to me. "Let me know when you're ready, Nicole," he said. Like a line from a movie or something.

And then he kissed me. No tongue or anything, just really soft, and I—I was basically melting and would have gone home with him immediately if not before but obviously that's not what he wanted. So he just dropped me here, and I said something—again—totally dumb, like thanks or see you or something. *Ugh.*

I've gone home with a lot of guys. But I've never had one wait for me to choose him. And all this time it irritated me that he didn't seem to want me, when it turns out he wants me, but only if it's for real.

How did he know? How did he know I wasn't ready for that before but maybe... maybe I'm ready now? Maybe I do want that. With him.

But fuck, it's a lot of pressure. He's a virgin FFS.

A virgin.

Why is that so hot?

* * *

RICKY KENDELL TO-DO LIST FOR FIRST DATE WITH NICOLE WINESAP

> make reservation at Spago
> buy new tie
> haircut

corsage? tennis bracelet?
special order a bushel of Winesap apples
~~condoms~~

* * *

From the journal of Nicole Winesap, age 20

I've never had sex with a virgin before. I don't know if I can do this. But we've been dating for months, and every time he kisses me I practically drench my... you know what I mean, and I know he wants me. He's just waited so long, and what if I'm not what he expected? What if I can't make it good enough for him? What if he's disappointed? He can't get a do-over.

My first time wasn't anything to write home about, but I was sixteen. Sex isn't supposed to be good when you're sixteen. Ricky's twenty. And he's adorable.

Okay, I like a challenge. I'll just make it really romantic. Maybe we should go to a hotel. But that might be too much. He has a bunch of roommates, so his place is iffy. I guess I could ask Rosie if she can stay with Kate for a night?

I've never wanted someone like I want Ricky Kendell. I refuse to screw this up.

We're having sex, dammit. And it's going to be the best first time in history.

* * *

Ricky Kendell, age 20, unsent text to Jamie Kendell, age 18, written, then deleted immediately after

RICKY

Sex is awesome, dude. Really lives up to the
hype. Ten out of ten. Do recommend. And
Nicole is… my everything.

* * *

FROM THE JOURNAL OF NICOLE WINESAP, AGE 20

Okay, Ricky Kendell is a fast study. I didn't even think he'd be
anywhere close to the best I'd ever had. It was his first time!
Come on. But at the moment, I'm so blissed out I can't even
remember the name of the guy who was formerly my best.

My man brought it.

I don't think I did too badly, myself.

* * *

RICKY KENDELL'S LIST OF PROS AND CONS OF MOVING TO NEW
YORK IF NICOLE DOESN'T COME WITH ME

> Pros
> get experience in related field
> live cheaply/save money
> make East Coast connections
> free for networking events
>
> Cons
> no Nicole

* * *

FROM THE JOURNAL OF NICOLE WINESAP, AGE 22

Ricky wants us to move to New York. *New York City*. He wants us to leave everything we know and everyone we love behind and move three thousand miles away. And that's not all. He wants me to apply to Parsons, for their industrial design master's program.

What the fuck am I supposed to do?

I love him, but this is a big step. We talked about moving in together after graduation, but I thought we'd get an apartment in Santa Monica or something. This is major. This is like... our future.

I don't think we'll make it if he goes and I stay. And I know he's going to go.

And yeah, I've always wanted to go to New York, to do the *Sex and the City* thing. But if I go with Ricky, I won't be a single gal on the town. We'll be figuring things out together.

Together. I knew Ricky was in this for the long haul, but I guess I didn't fully know what that meant.

I'm not sure about this. But I am sure that I don't want to break up.

I guess we're moving to New York.

* * *

FROM THE JOURNAL OF NICOLE WINESAP, AGE 24

Super tired. My manufacturing class is kicking my ass, but it's amazing. Ricky got an awesome end-of-year bonus, so he's treating me to a spa day this weekend. We're not going home for Christmas and my parents are pretty pissed, but I can't face flying at the holidays this year.

New York is so pretty right now. Yeah, it's cold, but the lights are so cheerful. All the store windows are decorated like crazy, and I'm so excited about my Christmas present for Ricky. I love him so much. And he was right about New York. We're building something here we couldn't have back in California. I know we'll go back someday, but for now, it's just the two of us against the world and I'm loving every second.

* * *

TEXTS BETWEEN RICKY KENDELL, AGE 26, AND BEN SMITH, AGE 26

RICKY

Congrats to you and Kate, man! Nicole told me you got engaged.

BEN

Thanks! I'm pretty lucky, right?

The luckiest.

You and Nicole ready for that step?

Ha. Well, we're working on it. There's no rush.

You sure about that? Nicole's not the most patient person in the world.

I've known she's the woman I wanted to marry since freshman year. But she has to be sure.

Good luck with that.

* * *

FROM THE JOURNAL OF NICOLE WINESAP, AGE 27

It's time to go home.

Our lease is up and Kate and Ben are getting married in a few months. Ricky's itching to start his own venture capital firm. I've been thinking about what I want to do. I've learned a ton working for other people, but I'm getting sick of having defer to their visions. I haven't touched my trust fund—Mom and Dad probably never thought I could actually support myself by working. Surprise! The money should be enough to set up my own shop. I just need a bit of space, some materials. Contacts I have in spades. Might be good to find someone to handle the business side of things, so I can concentrate on the creative stuff. A partnership?

I hope Santa Barbara is ready for the return of Nicole Winesap and all the fabulousness that comes with me!

* * *

FROM THE JOURNAL OF NICOLE WINESAP, AGE 27

Horrible, horrible news. Ben's dead. A traffic accident. We're flying to L.A. tonight to be with Kate. My heart is breaking for her. She's so strong, but I can't imagine what she's going through. She's terrible about asking for help, so I'm just going to stay with her until she's back on her feet.

My darling Kate.

Ricky's really shaken up. He and Ben were closer than I realized, always debating sustainability and ethical business practices and all that.

How can someone be here one day and then suddenly not?

What if I got that call one day? Ricky could get hit by a car, or shoved onto the subway tracks. Well, probably not, he never takes the subway, but something terrible could happen and what would I do then? He brings out the best in me. I wouldn't even know who I am without him. God, I'm freaking myself out. I wonder... maybe it's time that we stop playing house and actually go all the way.

We've talked about marriage, sort of hypothetically. I haven't been sitting around hoping he'll pop the question or anything, but things like this make you wonder what we're waiting for.

* * *

Texts between Ricky Kendell, age 28, and Jamie Kendell, age 26

RICKY

You're coming for Thanksgiving, right?

JAMIE

Wouldn't miss it, cuz.

You'll finally get to meet Ophelia.

Nicole's cousin, right? The young one?

She's 23. She's like Nicole's sister.

Strange we haven't met yet.

Well, you will on Thursday.

You're being weird about Thanksgiving. You're not going to propose over turkey and stuffing, are you?

What makes you say that?

I figured it would happen any day now. You guys are setting up here in Santa Barbara for good. You just bought a house together, for fuck's sake.

I'm not proposing at Thanksgiving at my parent's house, and I would appreciate it if you didn't talk about this subject with Nicole.

OK, OK. Touchy.

Everything okay with you two?

Of course. We're just not there yet.

Well, don't make her wait too long. She's not exactly patience personified.

I know what I'm doing.

* * *

FROM THE JOURNAL OF NICOLE WINESAP, AGE 28

Ricky and I had an amazing time in Napa for our anniversary. It was so romantic, and we needed the break from work. Lani and I have been pulling 12-hour days on Winesap Design and he's been down to L.A. and back a bunch of times for meetings, so we really needed to get away.

A part of me thought maybe he'd use the perfect setting and the freaking million-course dinner at The French Laundry as the opportunity to, well, propose.

It sounds kind of dumb written down like that.

It's not like I don't think we're going to be together forever. I just thought we'd reached a point in our lives when the inevitability meant we might as well take that last step.

Guess I was wrong.

* * *

FROM THE JOURNAL OF NICOLE WINESAP, AGE 29

My twenty-ninth birthday. Ricky went all out—we took a limo to the Bowl, saw Little Dragon, had a catered dinner from my new favorite place. Really excellent birthday.

And, oh yeah, he gave me a watch.
It's a really nice watch.
But where is my freaking ring???

* * *

RICKY KENDELL PROPOSAL PREP TO DO

> ask Nicole's parents for their blessing
> make sure ring is the right size
> get the champagne Nicole likes
> flowers
> L.A. Times announcement?

* * *

FROM THE JOURNAL OF NICOLE WINESAP, AGE 30

If I'm ever going to get married, I think I'm going to have to take matters into my own hands.

* * *

NICOLE WINESAP PROPOSAL TO DO LIST

> design Ricky's ring. size?
> ask his parents for their blessing? They love me already, but maybe?
> get that whiskey he likes
> flowers
> new lingerie? (why not)

* * *

RICKY KENDELL PROPOSAL SPEECH, DRAFT 16

Nicole, I've been sure about you from the start. I've never not known that you were the perfect person for me. And I wanted to be sure of you being sure about me right back.

I waited for you until I knew when I kissed you for the first time I'd be the last person you ever kissed.

When you chose to go to New York with me, we started to build the foundations of our future together. But we were still just kids playing around. Not with each other's hearts—no, you've never been cavalier with mine. Even so, it wasn't until we came home, bought our house, started building our businesses, that I knew we were working toward the same thing. Still, I waited.

I wanted you to be as sure about me as I've been since the moment I first laid eyes on you.

I love you with everything I am. You've made me a man rich beyond anything I could have ever dreamed of, not because of what abundance we have, but because with you by my side, I don't need anything else. You're enough. And I'm the luckiest man in the world to have the most gorgeous, most creative, most brilliant, most loving woman I've ever met be the person I get to spend my life with.

Will you spend your life with me?

Will you marry me?

* * *

FROM THE JOURNAL OF NICOLE WINESAP, AGE 30

I can't believe that just happened. What even did just happen?

I had it all planned out. I had a ring made. I had a speech

prepared. I was going to make steaks and baked potatoes and I bought a chocolate cheesecake. The bubbly was cold, and the whiskey was standing by. I was going to damn well take matters into my own hands and ask Ricky to marry me.

And I did.

I fumbled through the speech, but it amounted to the fact that I love him more than I thought I could love anyone, that I need him, that we're better together and I want to be together for the rest of our lives. Okay, that was better than what I actually said. Maybe I should have practiced a little more.

I pulled out the ring, and Ricky started laughing. Laughing! And then he left—he went to our bedroom, and I was about to hyperventilate but he came back before I could have a full-blown panic attack and he went down on one knee and showed me the ring he had made for me and he told me he wanted to wait until he was sure I was ready. He was, well, he was much more eloquent than me.

We put the rings on each other's fingers. It almost feels like we're already married.

Then we had sex on the floor of the living room and the baked potatoes burned to a crisp.

Anyway, I'm finally engaged!

I wonder how long I have to wait before I start planning the wedding?

ACKNOWLEDGMENTS

This is the fourth and final book in the Never a Bride series, and I'm so grateful for everyone who has come on this journey with me. It was a joy to spend so many hours with the fabulous, fearless Never a Brides, and coming to the final chapter of their story is bittersweet.

Thanks to Brian Calvert of Calvert Illustrations for the inspired cover designs, to Sue Khodarahmi and Sara Kettler for making the sentences shine, and to Pippa Baker-Rabe and Dylan Osborn for their support, both practical and emotional.

To my sprinting group—Arell, Isabelle, Nicole, DeLisa, Mary Ellen, Taylor, and everyone else. Thank you for keeping me in the chair and the words flowing!

To my plotting group—Kate, Isabel, and Annette. You inspire me and keep me on track. Thank you.

My Westport Writers' Workshop students give me so much joy, both as I share my knowledge of writing and publishing and as I'm inspired by their enthusiasm and beautiful stories.

Julie Bloomer, you have been unfailingly supportive of this series and my writing career, and I appreciate it so much. I love you.

The character of Reed is a children's book author and was inspired by my love of so many wonderful new children's series that being a mom has exposed me to. Some authors you should check out are Jane O'Connor, Mac Barnett, Jon Klassen, and Mo Willems, in addition to my personal classic favorites including Margaret Wise Brown, Robert McCloskey, and Barbara Cooney.

And thanks to Holden and Truman for always wanting me to read to you.

ABOUT THE AUTHOR

Libby Waterford is the author of the Sawyer's Cove: The Reboot and the Never a Bride series. She's obsessed with her pollinator garden, DIY fermentation, and writing swoony first kisses and hopeful happily ever afters. Her steamy contemporary romances mix witty banter and all the feels with a solid dollop of good old-fashioned sexual tension. Libby wrangles her two ever-growing sons and a husband in Fairfield County, Connecticut.

Get a free story at libbywaterford.com and email her at libby@libbywaterford.com.

facebook.com/LibbyWaterford

instagram.com/libbywritesromance

bookbub.com/authors/libby-waterford

goodreads.com/libbywaterford

amazon.com/author/libbywaterford

tiktok.com/@libbywaterfordauthor